Sh[...]d to withdraw as he tilted her chin up and sealed her surprised mouth with his own. The touch and taste of her stimulated him to bring up the matter of their marriage and their future.

She did not seem to share his own delight in their brief moment of passion.

"What concerns you my love? Can you be happy here?"

"You cannot support the extravagances of this estate on an income of two thousand pounds per annum."

He laughed. "Certainly not." The laughter faded quickly. "Why two thousand?"

She took a breath, licked her delectable lips, and blurted out, "Because that is my income per year."

Another Fawcett Book
by Ann Stanfield:

THE GOLDEN MARGUERITE

ROYAL SUMMER

Ann Stanfield

FAWCETT CREST • NEW YORK

Chapter One

As many of His Highness's household as could be spared from their tasks were gathered in the corridor of Everdene Hall when Lady Fiona made her way among them with her jingling gilt basket containing the miniatures of "suitable" British heiresses.

Like most aristocratic British households, the young ʼe's servants knew almost before His Highness did that he had been jilted by his beautiful cousin the Princess Eulalie (late of France and parts east) and he would now have to seek a bride elsewhere. It was devoutly hoped that a choice this time would have nothing to do with such commoner notions as "love."

The cook, Sarah Gimmerty, voiced the popular opinion. "He best look to the heavy blunt this time. Can't establish hisself in England on cream-pot love and a lady that's best at saucy head-turnings. Mark me. Prince Andre's hanging out for an heiress this time. Not but what he deserves the best, such a handsome lad as he is!"

Within minutes now, the whispers ran, His Highness would choose a life-shackle from among Lady Fiona's gaudy and probably inaccurate miniatures, not to mention her own full knowledge of every heiress making her come-out during this Waterloo year of 1815. In the tight-woven social world of the Prince Regent's London, Lady Fiona

Westerby would know such matters down to the last guinea and the last farthing.

Everyone felt that they could lay such matters securely in Lady Fiona's skillful hands. Among her other attributes, this slightly declassé lady always made herself popular with the staffs of the households she graced as a useful house guest.

She rapped discreetly on the cream and gold door of Prince Andre's music salon, then entered, though she hadn't heard his reply, if there was one. If he proved to be cross or on his high ropes, uncharacteristically conscious of his royal station, she would make the excuse that she had thought she heard his voice. Lady Fiona had been mistress to the prince's reprobate father and understood royalty very well.

She saw him standing at the long, splendid bay windows that looked out over the semicircular drive and the green expanse of lawn gently sloping away from the drive in three directions. His hands were tightly balled into fists behind his straight, trim back.

Perhaps he was remembering that all the rich Wiltshire property before him was still unpaid for. As Lady Fiona knew well, it had been acquired as proof to the Princess Eulalie that he could give her more than she might gain as the wife of a crabbed, eighty-five-year-old Yorkshire mill owner who was said to be as rich as Midas. The princess would be the old man's fourth wife, Samson Croft having easily outlived the other three.

But Princess Eulalie had chosen the Yorkshire Midas and was now plain "Mrs. Samson Croft," though, as she put it so prettily, "my friends will probably still address me by my title. From habit, you know."

Lady Fiona said nothing as she entered, but her evocative *attar of roses* scent had entered the room with her, and before he turned to acknowledge her low curtsy, he greeted her.

"Well, Fiona, are we now to blindfold ourselves and

choose at random some unlucky young heiress for a man whose pockets are to let?''

His tone was whimsical, but it did not fool Lady Fiona, who could read the pain in his dark eyes and note his control over warm and well-shaped lips that tightened slightly to conceal a very real emotion.

The new Mrs. Croft must have lost her senses to give up such a man as well favored as Andre-Charles de Bourbon-Valois. Considering his high pedigree in the Matrimonial Mart, he had a rare and delightful disposition. Her Ladyship liked a man with a dash of humor to season his exceptional good looks.

If I were ten years younger, she thought, but her own purse was certainly to let and her reputation as a worldly and experienced woman a trifle too well known.

No matter. She was quite enamored of another gentleman, not so high in rank, but plump in the pockets and of an almost absurd romantic disposition that caught her jaded fancy. Desmond Jasper might be bourgeois—his father had been a mere country squire and his mother a farmer's daughter—but he was the first man who had seriously taken her fancy since the death of Prince Andre's late and almost unlamented father.

Desmond Jasper would suit her very well. The thing was, she must maneuver herself into his orbit. Fortunately, the means were at hand, in the gilt basket with its miniatures of several likely heiresses, including Desmond Jasper's sister.

She countered the prince's frankness with a brisk pretense that what they were about to commit was a normal and even admirable act. She soothed any reservations with the thought that it was certainly normal, though not often admitted so frankly.

''I have a few trinkets, Your Highness, that may interest you. Portraits—''

''Of heiresses. I know. What a humiliating business!'' He turned away, then looked back at her, adding in fairness, ''Both to the young lady and to my family.''

She started to say something and he guessed her thought.

"I know. I have no family. The guillotine saw to that over twenty years ago. But to sell my name, my affections—not to mention the sufferings of the child I marry . . ."

Her wise, cynical eyes looked him over from his well-set dark head to his neat, fawn-colored pantaloons and worn but carefully polished boots.

"Forgive me, Your Highness, but I don't think we need dwell upon the young lady's sufferings."

His high-boned cheeks reddened. He avoided her eyes and especially the basket she carried.

"Lady Fiona, we are wasting time."

"Very true. Your Highness has always valued an honest statement of fact. Here is a very likely young female of good west country family—a Lady Clarissa Tremoyle." She paused long enough to observe with satisfaction that the sixteen-year-old child did not interest him. She had seen to it that the miniature revealed the most callow aspects of the young lady's face, not to mention a pout that hinted of willfulness. The next miniature was more hopeful in the prince's eyes, if not in Lady Fiona's scheme of things.

"Remarkably pretty. However . . ."

She coughed and pretended to study the miniature of a heart-shaped, big-eyed face in a cluster of golden curls.

"Hm. Yes. A pity."

"Pity?"

"It certainly isn't the fault of the young lady. One cannot choose one's ancestors."

"And what might be wrong with Miss—ah—Abigail Glenraven's ancestors?"

Lady Fiona consulted her memory with a great effort. "Oh, yes. It seems that Sir Mortimer Glenraven made certain accusations concerning the young lady's paternity. It is said he was foxed at the time. Within the year he withdrew his accusation."

She raised her eyes, stared at him innocently. She realized in this instant that His Highness was aware of her efforts to

4

sway his decision. She couldn't mistake the slight twist to his lips, the beginnings of a smile.

"Fiona," he challenged her frankly, "do you have a candidate in this charming bouquet?"

She blinked. "Not at all, Your Highness. I would never presume so much."

"Very well. Next?" But she was uncomfortably sure that he read her all too well. He seemed to be much more perceptive than his father had been.

She became flustered. "Miss Hannah—No. I'm sorry. The Honorable Maud Reeves is next. A most intelligent young female. A bluestocking, in fact."

Prince Andre put aside the forbidding portrait of the Honorable Maud, a lady whose eyes stared angrily out at the viewer beneath heavy, intimidating brows. He was looking as if he read Lady Fiona's mind and found it amusing.

"What seems to be the problem with the young female you cast aside? I believe you called her Miss Hannah—something?"

Lady Fiona had the grace to look embarrassed.

"No problem that I know of. Miss Jasper is most suitable."

"Your candidate, in fact."

"Only because she is a charming young lady. Neither empty-headed nor a bluestocking."

"Not a great beauty, then, and probably at her last prayers."

"Indeed not, Sir." Was he teasing her, or was he angry? She couldn't make certain just by his smile. "The young lady is not in her first youth, perhaps. She is past twenty-one. Not yet twenty-two, however. And very much sought after by her admirers."

Her forefinger pushed the miniature toward him, but perversely he refused to look at it. He still fixed those much admired brown eyes of his upon her, making her a trifle nervous, unlike her usual self-confidence.

He agreed with a sobriety that his amused smile denied.

"As old as that. Well, one must not expect a paragon. I take it that Miss—er—Jasper has a clouded family history. Relations who are not quite top-of-the-tree."

"Only one close relation, Your Highness. Captain Sir Desmond Jasper. Retired with honors. I believe he commanded a frigate against the French in the West Indies, where he received his wounds. She has a female companion of the usual sort. Quite unexceptionable."

The prince was observing her closely. She wondered if he sensed an unfamiliar excitement that enlivened her usually sophisticated features. After all, for a woman of thirty to be caught blushing like a schoolgirl was too absurd. He asked, "Our heroic captain is handsome, then?"

He must have noted what she had tried vainly to hide, that her real interest was in the brother.

"Tolerably. A big man. Quite unlike his young sister, who is slender and admired for her grace and—shall we say—her charm."

"I've no objection." He had tired of teasing her. Before she could draw the gilt basket away he reached in and took out five miniatures in their somewhat similar oval frames, one of pewter, two silver, and the others of various polished woods. He set them all on the big closed and locked pianoforte, then stepped back to study them from a slight distance. He found a covered harp standing behind him and touched the cloth covering for a minute, looking thoughtful. Lady Fiona was touched by the brief tenderness in his eyes before he again gave his attention to the heiresses lined up for his choosing. It was evident that he had been remembering the last time the strings of that harp had been plucked by the Princess Eulalie. It was hard not to remember the golden creature, leaning slightly forward, her soft lips parted, as she made the strings *thrum* and vibrate under her fingers: a beauty, and no mistake.

She would be quite wasted in far-off Yorkshire, but it would be better for Prince Andre if she remained in the North. Lady Fiona only hoped the latest gossip proved false. But the whispers were that Samson Croft might visit Bath for the waters, and Bath was much too near the prince's estate of Everdene Hall.

Prince Andre flipped aside pretty, yellow-haired Abigail Glenraven. "No blondes."

Evidently, he didn't wish to share the conjugal bed with a pale imitation of his beloved Princess Eulalie.

Possibly to further torment Lady Fiona, he considered young Clarissa Tremoyle and then a certain raven-haired Spanish beauty who hadn't come up in the conversation. He was really the outside of enough! After all this pretense and scarcely a glance at Hannah Jasper's pert face, attractive chestnut hair worn in the Grecian style, and her disconcertingly candid gaze, he ended Lady Fiona's torture by making this very choice.

"You knew it would be, *chérie*. Let us try our luck with the gallant naval hero's sister."

She could not help asking, "Has she really taken your fancy?"

He surprised her by his reasons. "She has a good mouth. Warm but firm. Not petulant."

"Oh, but a very handsome mouth, Sir. I mean to say . . ."

"It can be firm and still be handsome. She is certainly not an antidote. Actually charming, in an odd way." He looked at Lady Fiona. The humorous glint returned to his eyes. "It remains to be seen whether Miss Hannah Jasper finds a foreign-born prince equally charming."

She would be quite mad if she did not, thought Lady Fiona. "About the young lady's fortune. She has considerable command over her twenty thousand a year. During the late wars the Jasper Iron Foundries and other such investments were . . ."

"Later. Later." Obviously, he felt guilty at discussing his future bride's greatest attraction.

Still she persisted. "Sir Desmond, whose income is equally impressive, may be influential in the investment of her government funds. I have not been able to discover—"

This brought a bleak, ironic grin. "Is it possible there is something you have not been able to discover?"

He added then, and sternly, "I want no pressure brought to bear. No intimidation. If the young lady does not wish to be shackled to me, with all the formalities and boring ceremonials it would entail, she has my blessing and my permission to refuse. I shall tell her so."

"Yes, Your Highness. I quite understand. Incidentally, the young lady lives respectably but not lavishly in Bath. Quite near Your Highness's estate. Perhaps it is meant to be." She saw the impatient light in his eyes and added more rapidly, "It shall be as Your Highness desires."

She curtsied low, revealing half her ample bosom, tantalizingly pushed up by the high, tight waistline and more slender lines of her untrained Nile-green taffeta skirt.

He surprised her again by taking her hand and raising her from the curtsy.

"Dear Fiona, life is grim enough these days. Forgive me if I have a little fun at your expense."

"Always, Sir. I mean to say—Your Highness is much too kind. I only hope your bride is worthy of you."

"Well." He dismissed the matter easily. "Let us bag our little partridge before we ask ourselves if she is to our taste."

Chapter Two

"Stuff and nonsense," Miss Quilling sniffed. She had stopped in Bath's busy Milsom Street to make her pronouncement and her long, lean frame, holding the cane she wielded so dangerously, had diverted traffic around the bow windows of Mr. Smythe's Circulating Library.

Hannah Jasper was interrupted in her careful study of the library's interior and didn't for a moment realize what had set her companion onto this not uncommon tirade.

Miss Quilling pointed her cane toward the library. "In the past fortnight you have exchanged more books at this wretched shop than you ever read in your entire life. And what horrors!" The crook of her cane rapped the top novel in Hannah Jasper's arms, "*The Hand of Blood . . . Mysteries of the Night . . .* Will you tell me you actually enjoy such appalling trash? You had better taste when you were in your cradle."

Hannah laughed at that but was not shamed into satisfying the dear old pepperpot's consuming curiosity. She dared not go further along the street until she had managed to free herself of her dragon companion.

"Quilly, dear, do stop gabbling and help me. I must have a length of that pretty jonquil muslin on the counter in Humphries, the Draper's Shop. Enough for a walking dress. And satin lengths for a new opera cloak. Would you be an angel and attend to the matter for me? I'll just return these

9

books next door—unless, of course, you had rather. Here is one you didn't see—*Secrets of the Catacombs*.''

''Don't you pull a wheedle with me, my girl!'' Miss Quilling's long face lengthened further. But after a little thought she made a noise like *whoof!* and went her way into the draper's shop by the simple expedient of waving her cane. Two ladies, one of them the Dowager Duchess of Buccleigh, ducked instinctively and exchanged raised eyebrows before scuttling out into the street.

Satisfied that Quilly would be occupied for some time, Hannah Jasper hurried into Smythe's Circulating Library, a splendid room, worthy of the Regent himself, with its elegant crystal luster chandelier in the center of the main room, and sun pouring into the bookshelves from the bow windows. The anteroom beyond, dusty and shadowed, was her destination.

She passed without a glance novels of terror and romance, printed between cheap board covers, which were attractive to the majority of female patrons. Little knots of women had gathered around each stack of terror volumes, and Hannah dropped hers before little Mr. Smythe. They were immediately snatched up as she left the counter.

At the back of the shop, in the anteroom, a series of shelves revealed more books, this time large volumes of fact and scientific wonder. It was here that she found the person she wanted, whose presence would make Miss Quilling complain endlessly. The young man was dressed in the first style of elegance and leaning gracefully, if negligently, against the counter.

By what had proved to be a piece of good fortune, Mr. Beaufort Croft's common appellation of ''Beau'' Croft was not inappropriate. As Beau Croft would have confessed, it was his only good fortune, at the moment. Until his grandfather's surprise marriage to poverty-stricken Princess Eulalie of some petty principality in Central Europe, Beau Croft had been the presumed, if unstated, heir to Samson Croft's fortune.

Even the Beau's enemies, produced in part by his sharp gaming practices, agreed that his grandfather's marriage had been a wholly unexpected calamity.

One of the Jasper Woolen Mills ran cheek by jowl with Croft properties in the West Riding of Yorkshire, and Beau had been Hannah's playfellow in their youth. She had long ago decided that when her days of being paraded like a length of cloth before the eligible bachelors of the *haut-ton* were ended, she would probably marry her devilish and sometimes mischief-making companion. After all, she had once been a partner in the mischief of his youth.

She held out her gloved hands to him now, looking very nearly beautiful, with her bright smile and lively hazel eyes. She and Beau looked much more alike than she and her older brother Desmond, and she thought she could read Beau's mind upon occasion. It was often devious, but she could talk him out of most of his more wild escapades.

"Dear Beau, you really musn't take that marriage so much to heart. Your luck will turn. Very likely, that horrid princess will elope with the footman and you may be back in your grandfather's good graces again."

Beau's eyes widened a trifle at the sight of her in her fawn muslin walking dress with its golden-brown surcoat. They certainly brought out the matchless sparkle of her eyes, which were wider than his and less disillusioned. He took the hands she offered and neatly touched his lips to the uncovered inch of her wrist.

"You are in remarkably good looks today, Hannah. I take it that the Jasper fortunes have risen another thousand guineas."

She took a sharp breath and pulled her hands away.

"I wish you would not forever dwell upon fortunes, Beau. It makes you very tiresome."

He frowned, but he was used to speaking freely with this one reminder of a pleasant childhood.

"You'd dwell on fortunes quickly enough if you had none of your own. If only you had the free use of your fortune, or even your income, we could elope to the Continent and forget my damnable grandfather!''

She was aware that her lips pursed a trifle, the only sign of guilt, for she had lied to Beau, her dearest friend, leading him to believe her estate was entirely in the hands of her brother, Desmond. As though poor Des, with his head in the clouds so romantically, could ever manage her fortune! She had had the handling of it since she was eighteen. Even at fourteen she had known more than Des would ever know about stocks, government funds, foreign and domestic investments, and land speculation. She knew about ''cent-percents'' and borrowed money as well, though not from personal experience.

But she did not disabuse Beau of his belief that she was helpless to touch her estate. She had lent Beau sums out of her quarterly allowance in the past and known she would never see the money again. She didn't mind that, but she had not been so besotted over anyone that she would see her estate go the way of those quarterly sums.

She smiled suddenly at a memory of her own dear Des calling her ''Shylock'' because she refused to back some absurd fancy of his. As usual, it had been over a lovely female ''in thrall,'' as he put it, to her wicked protector, the owner of a neat little gaming house frequented by the bolder young spirits of the Regent's set. Des was always in the process of rescuing some fair damsel who possessed not a farthing to bless herself with, according to the damsel's own timid confession.

''Well, Beau, I haven't control of my money,'' Hannah lied glibly from long practice. ''So we must make the best of it. Now, do let's be friends again. Will we see you at the Pump Room tomorrow morning?''

He scowled at that. ''What? And meet every fusty old dowager in this benighted town? No one with any pretense to elegance comes here these days.'' But even aside from her fortune he enjoyed Hannah's company more than that of any female he had ever known. He could be completely himself with her, so he softened and volunteered, "I'll squire you to the Upper Rooms tonight and even waltz with you, if you insist."

"Thank you, Beau. You really are a dear—no matter what they say," she added mischievously.

He reacted as she knew he would. "What do they say? If they are complaining about my winnings at piquet with old General Titchloe, let me assure you there was mighty deep play that night and piquet was the least of it. If he claims I . . ."

"No. It wasn't General Titchloe."

"Then who . . . ?"

Again her smile warmed him. "You did. I am persuaded the general had no notion of your tricks. Rumor had it, your friend the general practices a few tricks of his own."

He stared at her, then slammed *The Practice of Self-Control* hard upon the counter.

"Damn, but I knew those cards didn't fall right! So he's a Captain Sharp. When I come upon him again, mark me, I'll be in better case to answer the sly old fox." He stopped, looked into her face and suggested whimsically, "You wouldn't, by chance, care to back me."

"Caught by my own petard," she murmured.

But he was already deep in his problems again. He returned to the main theme.

"If only I could show Grandfather Samson the real woman inside that pretty royal head of hers! He must be aware that he won her by a shower of golden guineas. It's obviously what captivated her."

"Unlike his grandson."

He grinned ingratiatingly. "Ah, but the difference is I know it— Speaking of the heavy blunt, you can imagine . . ."

"I know. I know." She emptied out her netted purse. She had come prepared for Beau's usual condition and carefully included the not inconsiderable sum of five guineas.

Instead of taking the gold coins his fingers hesitated. He

looked at her. "Someday, my good angel, I swear I'll repay you. It's only these bad times. I should never have quarreled with Grandfather. But the way he announced his marriage to me—damn! He knew what it meant. My entire future was cut up."

A disturbance at the wide front of the shop separated them both abruptly. Even without looking around, Hannah knew all the signs and sounds. She whispered, "It's Quilly. Don't let her know this was arranged between us."

"She hates me. Nothing but a shatterbrained old antidote, but she behaves as though I were a—"

"Hush! She can't refuse you if you arrive tonight in all your splendor."

"She will find a way. Gad's life! As though my poverty were some fault of mine. But Hannah, thank you. I'll repay you this time. I swear it. As the poets say, you are my heart's darling."

"Do hush. You know I dislike such twaddle."

"You sound more like Quilly every day. I wish you were a trifle more romantic," he complained. "There are times when a man could find you a real out-and-outer, if you'd let him."

"Well, I'm not and I won't. I have enough to deal with in Desmond's elaborate fantasies. And Papa's before him— Ah, Quilly. There you are. You were forever in the draper's shop. What detained you? Come along."

Hannah took one of Miss Quilling's long, bony arms and neatly turned her around, unmindful of the lady's grumbling.

"Wasn't that the Croft boy? The one who had his expectations cut up by that young foreign female? You know he is not the thing. Spends all his time in gaming halls." She ignored Hannah's pretended shock at the words and tried to look back over her shoulder, but Hannah moved forward persistently, under the candle lusters in the center of the Circulating Library and out to Milsom Street.

"You've known Beau Croft for this age, Quilly. Quite as

14

long as I have. He has been badly done by, and I only hope Mr. Samson Croft discovers what a greedy kitten he has taken to his heart.''

Miss Quilling laughed caustically. ''Say hearth, rather. Samson Croft has no heart. The girl is a beauty, they do say. It was ever the same. I recall when Samson and I were used to meet at the Assemblies—that was in the good days, my girl, when Bath was all the thing. Not like today, where you see nothing but invalids and half-pay officers from one day's end to the next.''

Having wandered off the subject of old Samson Croft, Miss Quilling raised her cane to signal the Jasper chairboys and got into her sedan chair, blocking the advances of a chair also being trotted up Milsom Street.

Inside the second chair a young woman sat forward and peered out. Hannah saw a mass of spun-gold hair peeping out of a fashionable *capote* hat festooned with pink ribbon rosettes. The face itself was worthy of a master-painter, with its exquisite complexion looking fragile as a rose petal, and great blue eyes gazing at the beholder, their beauty rivaled only by the sweetly tender mouth and slightly up-turned nose.

''Pardon, dear ladies,'' this gentle creature spoke in a charming accent, possibly French. ''Have I been at fault? My bearers did not see you. I shall scold them properly.''

Hannah was aware that her own pleasant, decisive voice sounded almost boisterous after that gentle whisper.

''Not at all, Ma'am. It was our fault entirely.''

The enchantress murmured, ''Too kind,'' and gave her two surprisingly hard-faced bearers the signal to move on.

''Now, who on earth may that be?'' Hannah asked Miss Quilling, but it was Beau Croft, standing quietly in the street beside Hannah, who answered her in a flat voice.

''That is none other than my dear, doddering old Grandmama Eulalie, Grandfather's royal bride.''

''Heavens, what a beauty! We shall all find ourselves in the shade if she is to remain here long.''

"Not you, Hannah." He shook his head. He was still looking after the chair with his eyes narrowed thoughtfully. "There must be more to that creature than those angelic airs she gives herself. If I approach her in the right way, she might help me to gain my share of the inheritance. Somewhere . . . somewhere, a clever man might find her Achilles heel."

She laughed. "I make no doubt that would be as beautiful as the rest of her."

Miss Quilling, seeing that she and her chair had left Hannah behind, stopped and waved her cane.

"Hannah, come along. You are delaying traffic. And tell that young man he had best arrive properly breeched tonight or he will never escort you to the New Assembly Rooms."

Beau Croft bowed low. "And good day to you as well, dear Miss Q."

Much amused, Hannah said, "Really! You two!" She warned Beau, "You had better come. There won't be another attractive male present, and I've no intention of waltzing with Samson Croft."

Then she strolled up the street after her dragon companion.

She had always liked the country. In many ways she preferred provincial Bath to the Prince Regent's hectic London and Brighton, but like most women, even sensible ones, she saw no reason why she shouldn't enjoy the company of an attractive young man.

In any event, it was good to know she could count upon one of those delightful creatures tonight.

Chapter Three

Miss Quilling said, "I do wish you would dress to your position. My dear, there are times when you quite put me to the blush. Puce is not the color for you."

Hannah wrinkled her nose at her. "I've had members of the FHC fall into flat despair when I wore brown and refused to stand up with them for the country dances."

"That's as may be. But everyone knows the Four Horse Club's creatures are fast, my girl." Hannah laughed at the unconscious pun but Miss Quilling pushed on relentlessly. "It's the waltz that should interest you, and as to brown, there are shades and shades. There is *fleur de terre,* and consider *rose du monde*—a dash of earth and sun there, and . . ."

Hannah paid little heed to these ramblings. Her abigail, Kitty, who was Miss Quilling's young, eager, terrified niece in training, brought out several other gowns from the old French armoire captured by Desmond from a French frigate, spreading them across the bed and chaise longue and even Hannah's delicate ebony desk, brought around the Horn from China. Hannah had never cared what she wore since her eighth birthday, when she overheard a conversation between the parents of two childhood comrades. She learned in one afternoon that her great attraction was the fortune bestowed upon her by a grandfather and a mother who knew quite well that her father would sweep through his own competence within a year.

This in no way lowered Hannah's high opinion of herself in most respects, but when a gallant admirer began to prose on about her "bright hazel eyes" and her "soft lips," she grew either impatient or uncomfortable and soon turned the subject, imagining that her admirer was "bamming" her, having fun at her expense.

"Well, then." She held a gold tissue overdress above her cream white satin gown and received the proper praise she expected from those she paid liberally. Their praise confirmed her confidence but did not in any way increase her opinion of her irresistable appeal. She knew better than that.

When she was dressed and had arranged her fine chestnut hair with careless abandon, a few curls about her cheeks, she attached her ruby set—the spectacular eardrops, the necklace of matched rubies on gold, and the ruby crescent against her hair. She felt that she had done the best she could with the material at hand. At the least, she would not embarrass her escort. Beau Croft's name was always coupled with the beauty of the moment, and she knew she had a lot to live up to.

"And will you be taking the captain's lovely gift, Ma'am?" asked Kitty who much admired Hannah's gallant brother. She put the new Cathay fan into her mistress's hand and Hannah spread it to admire the silken Chinese ladies who adorned the ivory sticks.

At almost the same time she heard the familiar heavy footsteps of her brother, Desmond, in the corridor outside her bedroom.

" 'Tis himself," Kitty cried, causing Miss Quilling to raise her scant eyebrows.

But Hannah was just as enthusiastic and called out, "Des, do come in. We weren't expecting you until tomorrow."

The big, sandy-haired man pushed open the long, white door and strolled in with a slightly rolling gait, as though still on the quarterdeck.

18

Captain Sir Desmond Jasper had made captain at twenty-four and been invalided out of the navy after valiant service against the French at Santo Domingo. In spite of his build, which was now muscular but could one day run to fat, he gave his acquaintance and loved ones a curious feeling that he was still naive and ingenuous.

His behavior bolstered that belief, since he was a perennial knight-errant. A female had only to make her appearance on his horizon weeping into her wisp of handkerchief looking helpless and he was off to tilt windmills for her.

At the age of thirty-three he was still unmarried, to the despair of young ladies in the marriage mart, not to mention their mothers. Hannah had promoted the interest of every friend she possessed in the hope of "settling Des down," but none of these females possessed the power to fix him permanently. He must be needed. He longed to be needed, to tilt windmills and perhaps carry off a fair lady on his saddle-bow. Up to this minute his quest for a *genuine* Beauty in Distress had been utterly vain, but his disillusionment did not last long.

He greeted his sister from across the elegant room with its chilly Empire beauty somewhat modified by the careless disarray of its owner, thanks to scattered garments, half a dozen pairs of silk-covered shoes, and innumerable spidery lace shawls to be worn draped over bare upper arms.

"I vow, that boy is like a gust of wind," Miss Quilling complained, but when Desmond Jasper strode by her and tilted her sharp chin with his bent forefinger, her severe and wrinkled features relaxed into what, in anyone else, might be called lines of fondness.

He lifted his sister clear off the floor in a hug, causing her to scold him laughingly, "Take care. You will ruin all of Quilly's and Kitty's work. Des, don't tell me you've gone and married that dreadful Carrigan woman from Tothill Fields."

"Lord, no. I saw through that fast enough when I met the

fellow who has her in keeping. 'Brother,' she called him. But there was no resemblance whatever."

"There is no resemblance between you and me," his sister reminded him, which only gave him pause for a few seconds before he waved away that detail while Hannah pulled herself together again.

"In any event, I wasn't taken in. Not after I met the 'brother.' Rough character. Fancied himself a pugilist." He rubbed his knuckles and blew on them.

The women looked at each other. Hannah voiced their concern. "You'll not be telling me you fought with him!"

He grinned, looking young and mischievous.

"Not much of a fight. Tried blackmail, and when I refused, he got between me and the door. Well, I couldn't allow that. Popped him a leveler to remember me by."

"Really, Master Des," Miss Quilling felt bound to put in while Kitty giggled, her eyes huge with admiration as she observed his physique, which was crowded into riding breeches, boots, and a six-cape coat he had already slipped back, giving his powerful shoulders more room to demonstrate.

Being of a practical mind, Hannah remarked, "At least you wasted no more money on her."

"Well, not precisely," Des admitted, looking a trifle sheepish. "The poor creature didn't have a feather to fly with, so I left her enough to keep her from . . . you know, the streets."

"How much?"

"Fif-fifty pounds."

Hannah rolled her eyes at Miss Quilling but was forced to laugh. She could only agree with Miss Quilling's summation.

"Master Des always had a good heart, my dear. Too late to bemoan it now."

"Never mind that. Des, go quickly and change. You may accompany us to the Upper Rooms like the dear brother you are."

He was not intrigued. "Fusty work! I didn't tool my chariot back to Bath in record time merely to spend the hours treading on toes at an assembly. You've enough admirers for that."

She tried one more gambit while Kitty draped her second-best opera cloak over her shoulders.

"Des, there is a princess in Bath. Married to Beau Croft's grandfather. Doesn't that sound romantic? A live princess?"

He shrugged. "One of those Frenchie princelings is about Somerset somewhere as well. They say he may be hanging out for a rich wife. That doesn't sound my sort of company, either. All that bowing and scraping. Can't get down to it. Breeches too tight."

The women laughed and Hannah kissed him lightly as she passed him on the way to the door.

"I do understand, dear. But fortunately, Miss Q. and I have an escort. Beau Croft is back in Bath, and he is always so obliging."

Des said, "Hmph. And you find my bits of muslin an expense."

All the same, he knew what was expected of him as his sister's only male protector. He shrugged back into his coat and followed the two women down the narrow, beautifully carved entry stairs to be certain they got off with an escort. The house itself was narrow, one of several similar houses built around the carefully fenced and vacant park of Queen Square.

The Jasper House on the south face of the square had been designed in the mid-eighteenth century to the exact specifications of a dandy with a taste for piquet who was forced to sell out at a loss. Through this means and to the horror of aristocratic neighbors, the charming little house came into the hands of Hannah's grandfather, referred to by his neighbors as a "jumped-up mushroom" and a "cit who had grown above himself."

But the overturn of ancient values in the French Revolution and the turn of the century itself had instilled in most of Jasper's Bath acquaintances a respect for the Jasper fortune, if not for the patriarch who had laid the foundation of that fortune on weapons of war, the new woolen mills, and speculation in the government funds.

Beau Croft had called at the Jasper house only minutes after Desmond's noisy arrival, and, knowing himself to be unpopular in that quarter, when Hannah crossed the entry hall into the delicate green salon he suggested, "We'd best be on our way. You know what a crush there is when all the Good Mamas make a push to enter at the same time."

"Much you care," she scoffed, aware that Miss Quilling muttered unflattering things behind her, just indistinct enough so that Hannah could not take offense.

But Beau, looking sleek and very much the gentleman in his immaculate eveningwear, complete with satin-smalls and silk stockings, assured her that tonight would bring out every dowager with a marriageable female.

"But why tonight, for heaven's sake?"

"Because royalty is flattering us with a visit. Unmarried royalty."

They went out and down the front steps together, Hannah curious in spite of herself.

"Not the Regent, surely. He has two wives, if we are to believe Mrs. Fitzherbert's admirers. I know! One of his brothers. Clarence? Cumberland? But all of them are so encumbered with children, legal and otherwise, that I shouldn't think the most naive heiress would want them."

Beau grinned wisely. "Not our own royalty. Ancient French, according to the gossip."

Suddenly, she recalled her brother's remarks about "princelings hanging out for a bride," and she knew Beau was right. Ambitious mothers, being at the opposite end of the scale from romantics like Desmond, were just as foolish, with far less kind hearts. A girl of good British stock would have to be mad to marry foreign royalty. Most of them were chinless, with large noses, and bound hand and foot by royal customs, traditions, and restrictions.

"Fascinating," she said. "How lucky I am to be in the company of such a brilliant escort! Otherwise, I should certainly fall victim to these princelings."

He grinned. "I am relieved. I shouldn't like to lose your regard."

"Charmingly put."

"Because I am used to it, you know."

"Odious creature," she murmured sadly. "My hopes are entirely cut up. I thought it was my personal attractions that won your regard."

"And so it is. The granddaughter of Old Midas Jasper must always hold charms for me."

Hannah laughed, but Miss Quilling, shocked by such appalling frankness, interrupted with the reminder "You are keeping the poor chair-boys waiting. Have some compassion. The night is growing brisk."

"Oh, Quilly, a good walk up the hill would put us all in spirits."

"And ruin our shoes in the bargain. Or would you prefer to wear iron pattens through the filth of the streets."

Hannah resigned herself. "Very well. But it is positively gothic. I must speak to Des about ordering a smart carriage for us, or lending me his phaeton. Heaven knows, he is an abominable whip, and I'd as lief tool a coach myself as have his hands at the reins. But his London curricle might serve me very well here in Bath."

"And have the wretched horses forced to mount the Gay Street Hill every day or so?"

Hannah's attachment to animals was said by some love-lorn suitors to exceed her attachment to mankind and she apologized.

"No. I shouldn't like that. One is a fool to ride in Bath when the walk is infinitely more pleasant."

"Well, come along, then. The chair-boys have been waiting this age, as if you were Queen Charlotte herself." Miss

Quilling motioned to the young chair-boys, who hurried to assist Hannah into the sedan chair. As was often the case in dealing with Hannah, they were just an instant too late. She seated herself in the rented chair without help.

With Beau walking beside Hannah's chair, they all started up the hill through the summer darkness toward the New Assembly Rooms. The town after sunset slightly resembled a medieval walled city. Footpaths were not so plentiful here as in busy London, so anyone traveling through the deserted streets, lighted by an occasional lamp or flaring torch, was glad to reach his destination.

For once in her life Hannah did not share this general feeling of anticipation. She enjoyed dancing as she enjoyed the company of her friends, but there were moments like this when she asked herself if her life would forever be circumscribed by these tame moments with her old friend Beau when, beyond the boundaries of her tiny world, there were dashing men behaving with shocking abandon toward young women her age who enjoyed it.

She knew she was not a romantic, nor ever had been, but surely, somewhere, there must be a few males out of the common way who could overset all her notions of propriety and at least try to sweep her off her feet.

She sighed. Obviously, they would not be found tonight at the highly proper and well-chaperoned Upper Rooms.

Chapter Four

The building that housed the New Assembly Rooms, the scene of balls, routs, card games, concerts, and assignations among the polite world, was a solid, somewhat oppressive stone building perched on a height near the Bath stone Crescent, Circus, and other elegant neighborhoods with their residences shoulder to shoulder in closest harmony.

The Jasper chair-boys loped over the cobbles to the New Assembly Rooms, popularly called "The Upper Rooms," just as several equipages, ignorant of the polite custom against carriages and the danger to teams, jockeyed for position at the front and side of the building. While Hannah sat forward, gathering her skirts and reticule, making ready to step out, Miss Quilling pushed the worn bit of curtain aside and peered out of her own chair, frowning.

"Something seems to have brought out every dowager in Bath. Indeed, we are deluged by hopeful young females." She nodded wisely. "You may lay it to the rumors about that tiresome Prince Andre."

Beau remarked with suitable cynicism, "I daresay His Highness will make a royal appearance at the witching hour."

"I don't advise it," Hannah laughed. "The poor man will be forbidden the door. Even a prince would find it impossible to break the eleven o'clock closing rule."

However, Miss Quilling had not made allowances for the

Jaspers' intrepid chair-boys. They were already shuffling forward, within the narrow confines between the Chillingworth team and a curricle in which a smart young London dandy had expected to cut a dash among what he was now calling loudly, "a pack of dowds and fubsy-faced females."

Within two minutes the chair-boys set the chairs down. Holding his hand out to Hannah as she stepped out, Beau remarked with the bitter undercurrent he hid from everybody but his childhood confidante, "How great is the power of the Jasper fortune! Even your servants are able to nudge aside all obstacles."

"Beau, if you persist in talking such fustian, you are no friend of mine. Take Quilly's arm. She may appreciate your tragic airs. She is a romantic. I am not."

Beau Croft looked as if he would like to follow her advice, at least to the point of deserting her, but after obeying her to the point of depositing Miss Quilling beside her in the doorway, he let himself be received into the bright, crystal-lighted interior of the Upper Rooms as her respectable escort. Perhaps he suspected, as Hannah did, that he might no longer be quite so welcome if he entered that select interior alone.

Making their way through the much talked about Octagon Room, where a few inveterate card players had already gathered, they arrived in the crowded ballroom, with its impressive chandeliers, whose sparkling crystal gleamed with splendor. The ballroom's most expensive ornament, however, was not the chandeliers, nor the splendid columns, nor the high ceiling, but the dowagers gathering in little clumps or seated upon the benches against the wall, dressed in all their jewels and hoping to parade their daughters, nieces, and other charges before the equally splendid assortment of eligible males.

The eager or shy young prospects, for the most part girls too thin or too stout for the mode, all shared one attribute. They possessed the financial status that gave them the title of "heiress," or even better, a family tree that traced itself sufficiently far back to permit their being eventually received at court by old Queen Charlotte.

Hannah Jasper knew many of the young ladies because their doting Mamas trusted her. Her own shocking freedom to manage her financial affairs was known to few of the hopeful dowagers, and they had long ago accepted her as an unlikely rival of their own daughters, being too frank, "too coming," and luckily, no beauty.

Despite these flaws, or perhaps because of them, Hannah remained popular with these young ladies as well, several of whom fluttered across the expansive floor in the wake of the Master of Ceremonies, to greet her.

This exalted personage, a gentleman of unexceptionable family and faultless manners, came forward, confiding with an arch air of mystery,

"Miss Hannah, you will not credit our good fortune tonight. We may—" He rose on the toes of his carefully polished evening boots for emphasis. "We just may be honored by a visit from His Royal Highness Prince Andre-Charles-Louis de Bourbon-Valois, a recent happy resident of our countryside."

She did not know why this announcement should annoy her so much, except that it was growing more tiresome with each repetition.

"Is that why we are so thin of male company tonight? I confess I find an Assembly-Ball a trifle flat when there is a lack of partners."

Beau laughed and promised her, "When the first set is formed I shall do my best to mend matters."

As if to deny his own promise, he was seized upon at that minute by two young men who, though carefully dressed in correct breeches, silk stockings, and elegantly reserved black coats over livelier waistcoats, coaxed him to join them in the cardrooms. He made an apologetic moué to Hannah and departed.

She wondered briefly if it was her own five guineas he

was risking, but she was beseiged by two eager, chattering young ladies and could not in politeness stop to tease Beau on the subject of his losses.

The Master of Ceremonies gave up his efforts to interrupt this artless prattle. He was well aware that several gentlemen standing around the long room under the dazzling lights had Miss Jasper as their object, so he need not trouble to provide her with a partner. He bowed and proceeded to a less favored young lady with an even greater fortune whom he might oblige in a similar way.

Sixteen-year-old Clarissa Tremoyle, a lively little brunette with pansy-violet eyes and a roguish disposition, noticed Hannah at once. "I mean to set my cap at the prince, you know. Princess Clarissa! It has such a ringing sound. Like the abbey bells. Most suitable, you will allow."

Hannah's eyes sparkled with amusement. The little orchestra was tuning up, and the scrape of a violin made her look quickly in the direction of the musicians just as a golden-haired young man, Albert Chillingworth, delicately handsome and highly eligible, broke from the observant males across the room and approached the nosegay of beauties around Hannah. Caught by her ease and the delightful laughter in her eyes, young Chillingworth abruptly presented himself as a partner to Hannah instead of to Clarissa, whom he had intended to squire into the set.

Half an hour later, having been led out to make one of the next set as well, Hannah found herself beside Clarissa Tremoyle as they came off the floor after a brisk *boulanger*. Clarissa pointed out a woman of thirty or so just entering the ballroom on the arm of a stout, red-cheeked gentleman whose breeches and coat seemed tight despite the fact that he obviously wore stays to contain his stomach.

The woman was handsome and red-haired. Her green gauze dress and silk undergown, with its slight fullness in the skirt, and her spider-lace shawl all indicated a lady of the Regent's Carlton House circle; yet there was a something about her, accentuated by the voluptuous display of at least half her flawless white breasts that made Hannah understand when Clarissa murmured,

"Oh, famous! That must be Lady Fiona Westerby. The *on dit* is that she was the mistress of Prince Andre's father. She cuts quite a dash, doesn't she? I heard Mama say she hoped to play the same obliging role for Prince Andre but he won't come up to scratch."

Hannah said, "From the look of him, I should say Lady Fiona is well quit of that family."

Clarissa studied Lady Fiona's fat companion with disappointment. "No. You cannot be in earnest. *That* is the prince?" She sighed. "It is always so. Look at the new king of France. They say he can hardly get about with that great . . ."

"Belly?"

She was overheard and saw herself eyed with disapproval by the Dowager Duchess of Buccleigh, who had just arrived with her granddaughter, an exceedingly plain child with an unfortunate complexion. The girl seemed terrified of the duchess, not without reason.

The duchess, however, had made the Jasper family her target. "Miss Jasper, you are aware, I collect, that your brother is making a disturbance out in the street. He has a wretched hand with horses."

The observation was undoubtedly true, but Hannah did not like to hear any criticism of Des, so she said defensively, "No doubt he was provoked."

She hurried past the imperturbable usher and out to the portal, where Desmond, with his usual heedlessness, had managed to tangle the wheel of his high-perch phaeton with the lower wheel of a four-horse carriage. None of the six delicate, highly bred horses should have been involved on these hilly, cobbled streets, and Des, in particular, knew better.

A trim young man in a coachman's many-caped greatcoat began to disengage the wheels while he ordered Desmond, "See to your horses, you fool."

How tiresome of Des to run into anything as large as a heavy, four-horse carriage! The young coachman had good reason to be impatient.

Des puffed and fumed as he reined in his plunging animals. It was perfectly clear that he would have been more at home fighting the French off Santo Domingo. Hannah hurried out to shout at him.

"Des, for heaven's sake, do as you are told! You are cow-handed with those poor creatures. Let me have their handling."

She tried to make her way between the two teams, but the young coachman put out an arm, providing an unexpected barrier.

"Wait. You will stain your gown. I'll attend the matter."

Though slender, the coachman had strength and a certain ability with horses. He got the reins from Des with surprising ease, and almost immediately the frantic horses were subdued. They settled down to quiet trembling under his hand as he slapped their flanks and spoke to them softly, words Hannah couldn't quite make out.

At the moment it seemed that Des needed her more than his team did. He leaped to the ground, disheveled and looking foolish, his big frame half out of his travel cloak and carefully fitted swallowtailed coat. Hannah only wished she had failed to understand his words, but unlike the young coachman, his language was all too clear.

"Damnable lubberly cattle! I've seen press-ganged widgeons with more sense."

"Des! Recollect yourself. You aren't at sea now." She smoothed his coat over his powerful shoulders, threw his cloak over his arm, and patted his hand. "You look splendid. All the young ladies will adore you. Incidentally, you might be kind to Miss Eliza Buccleigh. The duchess has been fire-eating again." She reminded him with a smile, "Very like you, my dear. But poor Eliza badly needs rescuing."

He brightened at a memory. "Muffin-faced little creature, as I recall, poor soul. But a kindly child. I'll try and cheer her.''

"No one can do so better than you, dear. Go along. And in heaven's name, don't tell anyone that I was out here.''

"Certainly not." He was indignant at her sisterly view of his discretion. "But why aren't you coming with me?''

"I have a word to say to the coachman. I'll be along.''

By this time an ostler had taken Desmond's phaeton and team under his capable charge.

Des hesitated, but Hannah pushed him as a hint, and he left her, muttering to himself. She had never questioned the matter, but she was aware that her ability to order her older brother's life was astonishing to all who knew them. She had frequently dismissed the point with the observation that any woman of character could do the same. Her private hope was that a woman of character should deserve him. His explosive temper might alarm the casual observer, but he was a lamb in his dealings with women.

She turned to the coachman, preparing an apology and explanation for Desmond's conduct, but the young man seemed amused by her own recent conduct.

"Your husband, Ma'am? I am not surprised that you had such sure hands with his team.''

She was offended by the implication, but she recognized its truth. "I'm afraid I've grown accustomed to treating Des as a very dear little brother.''

"A little brother?''

His eyes widened. By the flickering light of the coach lamps she saw that they were handsome eyes, warm and dark, with a little glint of humor. She wondered why it should surprise her that a coachman was so attractive and so young, but every coachman in her experience had been crabbed, gruff, and much older than this young man.

Whatever this unusual coachman's appearance, she felt her brother deserved a defense.

"My brother was decorated for his heroism at Santo Domingo. He is the bravest man I know." This had very little to do with the matter at hand, but she was anxious that no one think Des remained under her thumb.

"Brave? I am persuaded that he is," the young man agreed seriously, but the humor was there, in his eyes and the twist of his warmly sensuous mouth.

"No. I mean—although he is over ten years my senior, he has a very romantic nature. Quite unlike me."

"Really!"

"And he is forever in the suds over any female . . ." She collected herself. She was speaking to a servant and a stranger. "Anyone who seems in need of rescuing."

The young man appeared fascinated. "Rescued from what, may I ask?"

"From . . . life."

"I see. That is certainly comprehensive. And you, in turn, rescue him."

"Just so."

"He is uncommonly lucky to possess so useful a guardian angel."

She colored faintly, wondering that this coachman, servant to one of her friends in the ballroom, should openly express such amused contempt for her, and she drew herself up to give him a freezing setdown. But something in his eyes besides humor seemed to suggest that he regarded her with either liking or admiration, perhaps both. He was a novelty, in his profession or out of it, since men with his looks and charm were not in the common way. Nor was she immune. She remembered her lament earlier in the evening, that men out of the common way never seemed to cross her path. She amended her first intention.

"I have my brother's protection as well as his devotion. He is very dear to me. Meanwhile, I will leave you to your task or your mistress may scold you for loitering."

"My mistress?"

She explained impatiently, "The lady, or the gentleman, who employs you."

Belatedly, he seemed to comprehend, but of course, he

had known at once what she meant. He was merely having fun again at her expense. Probably his unusual looks and that winning manner had made him spoiled. A pity.

But he did have charm.

She returned to the ballroom, where she found everyone in a pelter over her disappearance. Beau asked to see her privately, warning her, "The devil's in it, Hannah. I've gone down ten guineas. I'll lay my life there were deep doings among them, but not by me, I'll swear!"

Miss Quilling burst in upon this whispered plea to demand that Hannah "look to yourself, girl, when that young man cuts a wheedle. You cannot be forever rescuing him. Mark me, your generosity merely encourages him."

Clarissa Tremoyle's high young voice cut through the clamor.

"Oh, Hannah, that Lady Fiona—you know, the late prince's mistress—is coming with the Master of Ceremonies. I'll wager she asks one of us to stand up with His Highness."

Hannah glanced across the ballroom, saw Lady Fiona's stout male companion bow to her, and pretended not to see him. After the curiously exciting episode with the young coachman, she was in no mood to be obliging and subservient with a fat prince who was clearly hanging out for a rich wife. She turned away with Beau, leading him toward the tearoom, where they found her brother's friend Colonel George Forbin vainly searching for her, his hands fully occupied in balancing tea and a plate of cakes. She begged his pardon, said privately to Beau Croft, "I have barely more than the change of one guinea in my reticule. You may have it but that is the end. Am I clear?"

Beau nodded, his dark face lightening. "Dearest Hannah! No more. After tonight I shall hedge off. Word of honor."

Aloud, she said as she gave him her pearl-beaded reticule, "Will you hold this while I drink my tea?"

"A pleasure, Ma'am."

She did not look at him. She was busy taking the tea and a

macaroon from the plate the colonel presented, just as Lady Fiona tapped her shoulder lightly with her fan. On closer view, the woman was a trifle older than she appeared at a distance, and though her hair was piled high, with a diamond-studded plume to accentuate the red-gold of its color, Hannah suspected the hair color received some aid from one of the well-known coloring agents now available. No matter. She did have a pleasant, worldly-wise smile.

"Miss Jasper, I have enlisted the aid of this good man." She indicated the Master of Ceremonies. "He has offered to present me to you. I am commanded by His Royal Highness to ask if you will honor him when the dancing begins again."

While everyone within hearing stared in disbelief, Hannah made her polite but definite refusal.

"I do not dance tonight, my lady. I have a . . . a headache. I will be leaving shortly. Please express to His Highness my sense of the honor he has paid me and my deep regret."

"Oh, but I am certain . . ." Lady Fiona persisted, leaving Hannah nothing to do but ask the colonel, "Would you oblige me with your arm? And summon the chair-boys for Miss Quilling and me?"

The colonel, too, sputtered in surprise. He was an attractive, likable man of forty who had aspired to her hand since she was seventeen, but even he did not rate his company higher than that of royalty.

She hadn't intended to leave so early, but the evening, like bad champagne, had gone flat. Besides, she rather wondered if the young coachman might still be out on the cobblestones when she left the building.

He was not.

Chapter Five

Desmond Jasper's uncommonly happy arrival home in Queen Square that night was in decided contrast to his sister's last sight of him outside the New Assembly Rooms some three hours earlier.

He burst into her warm, cozy boudoir now after the merest scratch on the door to announce his presence. "Hannah, I have seen her."

He swept across the room as if blown by a nor'easter up Halifax-way, and hugged his sister. Hannah, long used to his exuberance, kissed his weathered but not unhandsome cheek and motioned him to be seated on the blue satin-covered chaise longue, which creaked under his weight. She took the comb and brush from Kitty's hands and began to comb her hair more or less unconsciously while she looked at him. He seemed to be bursting with excitement.

"Yes, dear. I understand. That is to say, I don't understand precisely. You have seen her. Who?"

"The princess, Hannah. The princess."

"What? The heir to the throne, here in Bath? That will put a spoke in the Regent's wheel. Prinny with his eternal Brighton this and Brighton that."

"No, you silly goose. Not our Princess Charlotte. The other one. Princess Eulalie. Old Samson Croft's bride."

"Oh. That one. I very nearly was presented to her beloved tonight. I confess I was not impressed by him, so I pleaded illness and came away. As a matter of fact, I met a coachman-groom who was a deal more attractive. So you see?''

Desmond frowned. ''Well, we all know Old Samson. He gave me a monstrous scold because I climbed over one of those York stone walls when I was five or so. Even set his dogs on me. Remember? I made a run for it.''

They were talking at cross-purposes, and Hannah had to cover a yawn before explaining, ''Not Mr. Croft. That prince who is hanging out for a bride. And I may say, the excitement over him is incomprehensible to me.''

''Didn't come in his way. It's this Princess Eulalie. I had no notion anyone could be so fragile and delicate. Like a golden sunbeam . . . an exquisite, silken butterfly. And gentle. You'll not credit this. She stood up with me in the country dances.''

Moved as usual by his dear humility and longing to puff him up to a sense of his own worth, she put a hand out to him.

''My dear, it was she who was honored to be chosen by you.''

He was pleased but waved aside such nonsensical sisterly prejudice. ''Gad's life, girl, she is a princess, I tell you!'' He lowered his booming quarterdeck voice to confide while Miss Quilling and Kitty leaned closer to hear, ''But I've a strong suspicion that wretched old monster is already mishandling her.''

Hannah tried to express her skepticism lightly. ''The bride needs rescuing already?''

He scowled and slapped his substantial thigh.

''Hannah, have you no compassion in you? You are pitiless. That child, that . . . that frail, lovely creature was forced to accept the revolting embraces of a man old enough to be her—'' He recollected his company and broke off hurriedly. ''But enough on that head. I should not be discussing such matters with ladies who have never . . . who . . .''

''With maiden ladies?''

"Precisely." He stood up, leaned over his sister, and dropped a mere sketch of a kiss on her forehead. "Enough for tonight. Perhaps later, when you have had time to reflect on your . . . your : . ."

"Compassion?"

"Just so." He pinched Miss Quilling's cheek, grinned at Kitty, and left the room. He was humming again. They heard him all the way to his bedchamber.

Upon one reason or another he was up at six and out for a stroll before his sister finished her early-morning tea. Since his habit while ashore was to sleep late, Hannah was a trifle concerned over this sudden change in him. As she had suspected, his thoughts were still fixed upon Mrs. Samson Croft, the former Princess Eulalie. He broke in upon Hannah in the breakfast parlor with the princess's name upon his lips.

This time, however, he was accompanied by a good audience, his friend and crony, Colonel George Forbin, with whom he spent hours arguing the navy versus the exploits of the Peninsula Veterans.

The colonel behaved with his usual gallantry toward Hannah, taking the hand she offered, squeezing it in his friendly way, and then bowing low and bringing it to his lips as though he had only just thought of the gesture.

Still, even the colonel, who had been her hopeful suitor for so long, appeared to be excessively concerned with the former princess. While saluting Hannah's fingers in his accustomed way, he went right on answering Desmond's effusions.

"No doubt of it, Old Chap. Never met a lovelier creature—present company being excepted, naturally."

"Naturally," echoed Hannah with a wry smile.

Des grinned too. "You made a handsome retreat, George. All the same, you can't deny that Her Highness is quite the loveliest creature you've ever seen." His mood darkened. He chewed up a slice of Hannah's toast thoughtfully. "She has such delicate hands, and I thought I made out a black and blue mark across her right knuckles when she removed her glove that time. If that old ogre has been mishandling her already, there is no knowing how far he may go. I tell you, it set my blood boiling.''

Hannah felt that she needed fresh air and sunshine. She knew herself to be uncharacteristically ruffled by what appeared to be the universal adoration of the former Princess Eulalie. There had been beauties visiting Bath before, but none who turned the male population so topsy-turvy as Samson Croft's bride.

The day was warm but breezy, much more refreshing than the sullen, gray weather of the past week, and perfect for a good stroll. She might even wander up around the Crescent and catch a glimpse of the new Mrs. Samson Croft. She could not imagine why she should make it an object to view that paragon among women again, but her curiosity had been aroused.

Then, too, she remembered the Samson Croft of her childhood when she and Des stayed the summers with Grandmama Branshaw. He had been what Papa called a typical moorland dweller. Rough, sharp-spoken, but honest and, in his way, proud. Samson Croft had been amused by what he called "your courage, luv." He had been an ugly old man even then, physically powerful, but when he met Hannah unexpectedly on the village path across the moor, she pretended not to be frightened like the other children of the neighborhood, and he had liked that. Once, in the village, he had given her a square of gingerbread, which he called "moogin." Des refused to eat his moogin, but Hannah felt this would be impolite. Besides, she found it delicious. The old man had smiled grimly and patted the top of her head.

And now, years later, old Croft was thought to have mistreated his fragile bride within weeks, scarcely more than days after their wedding. Knowing Desmond, Hannah suspected he had been swayed by his fanciful and romantic imagination. Not to mention his own jealous desire for the lady. It hurt a little that Hannah's persistent and faithful suitor, George Forbin, had joined the admirers of the ex-princess, but she shrugged off this truth while changing to a simple blue-figured muslin gown and a Norwich shawl, which would protect her from the hilltop winds.

At the last minute she remembered to wear one of her bonnets. Not the most fashionable in the world, the blue satin ribbons being a trifle faded and the plume modest, but it would serve. Normally, she was indifferent to the opinions of casual acquaintances, and she much preferred the summer breezes in her hair, but on the chance that she might encounter either Mr. or Mrs. Croft, she wanted to be thought a lady, and not a bonny milkmaid.

She started out from Queen's Square and up the gravel path under the trees, walking rapidly, exerting herself against the petulant jealousy that had sent her out of doors. She was not accustomed to such feelings nor, indeed, to this strange, unsettled boredom with her life.

Once she left the environs of Queen's Square, with its early-morning peddlers of milk, summer berries, fish, and oddments needed by the various households, Hannah found herself nearly alone.

Ahead of her, at the far end of the magnificent Bath stone crescent, the color of rich honey, she saw a man and woman standing on the steps before the last doorway. He held the reins of the black mare who showed signs of impatience. Perhaps the man was a groom. The slender female, her face concealed by a fashionable plumed bonnet, descended the steps, went through the iron gates, and patted the mare. She murmured something to the horse, ignored the groom, and hurried back inside the house.

The man turned away and began to walk the black mare.

Hannah started around the Crescent, wondering which of the doors concealed her brother's ogre, Samson Croft, and his wife. Possibly, the woman in the bonnet was Eulalie Croft. With rising curiosity Hannah stepped back to get a better look at the windows above her on the first floor. No one seemed to be visible, until she caught a glimpse of the curtains moving at one of the windows in the last residence. The woman who had been talking to the groom now watched him from what looked like one of the drawing rooms.

Hannah winced as she put her weight on a pebble in her flat-soled moroccan slipper. Even her credit could be severely tried if she removed her shoe here before any possible watchers at those windows. She limped away from the Crescent with difficulty, hoping no morning stroller would see her on the path under the trees.

She reached the pebbled ground, leaned against a tree trunk, and untied the ribbons of her shoe. She tapped the shoe against the tree and set it on the ground. Balancing on one foot she teetered a moment, trying to slip her foot into the shoe. She would have succeeded at once, but she was startled by the careful drop of hooves, gentle but unmistakable.

She jerked her shoe back, fell against the tree, and saw the black mare calmly led around her by the man she had seen earlier across the Crescent. At this close vantage point she recognized him at once as the handsome young coachman she had seen last night at the New Assembly Rooms.

Hurriedly, she dropped the flounces of her skirt and stepped into her shoe, trying at the same time for a show of nonchalance.

"A pebble." Not very creative, and the young man smiled. He stopped walking the mare, who had turned her head, regarding Hannah with a snort of impatience.

The young man apologized charmingly. "You must forgive Zephine. She is jealous of other females."

Hannah said, "I know precisely how she feels," which made the young man laugh.

"Your pardon, Ma'am, but if you are in difficulties with your foot—Zephine may be persuaded to carry you to your lodgings."

"I should not dream of putting her to that trouble." The groom was studying her with those alarmingly attractive eyes, making her conscious that she was not in her best looks. At the same time it occurred to her that in all her life she had never concerned herself with a servant's opinion of her appearance or even her conduct. The thought disturbed her. She was not used to finding herself at a disadvantage. She felt that she must explain her presence here.

"Such a lovely day! I am fond of a good, stiff walk upon occasion, but I did not allow for these tiresome pebbles."

"Annoying. But the view is superb."

He had been looking at her, and she was about to bristle at his impudence when he gestured over his shoulder at the city of Bath, spread artistically below them on the hills and valleys around the River Avon.

She agreed quickly. "I've always thought so. I have a great fondness for Bath and Somerset. In part, that is why I walked up here today."

"In part." He ran his hand over the shining black flank of the impatient mare.

Feeling foolish but refusing to hide behind a lie, she confessed, "I was curious to see Mr. Samson Croft's new bride. I am told he has taken a lease upon one of the Crescent houses."

His smile died. "Yes. The last in the ellipse."

So her first suspicion was true. The lady she had seen with him a few minutes ago might well be the celebrated princess herself. Which put this young man in the service of Samson Croft.

"Good heavens! Was it the Croft team I saw you handling last night? I have known Mr. Samson Croft his age." She patted the mare's withers. "Then this beauty is Mrs. Croft's mount. I must say, Mr. Croft was never thought to be such a good judge of horseflesh."

"No," he agreed, curiously somber now. Even his pleasant smile seemed to be forced. "Zephine was chosen by Her Royal—that is, by Mrs. Croft." He added after a slight pause, "I was present, of course."

"I envy her," Hannah said lightly. "To have found such an animal. Not in Bath, I imagine."

"No. From London. Tattersall's."

"Yes. That was obvious." She patted the horse again, knowing she should not be seen here on a public path conversing with a stranger, a coachman-groom who was not even in her employ. She had always regarded herself as broadminded to a fault, but even her credit would not stand against a whisper that she was fast. Not even fast women of her set spent time in conversation with male strangers more properly employed in the stables, nor were they her stables.

"Do you ride, Miss Jasper?"

"When I am in London. Occasionally here on paths off Camden Crescent and to Beechen Cliff with my brother or Colonel—or my friends." She raised her chin, knowing she should not be so quick to satisfy his curiosity. "I am said to be tolerably skilled, though perhaps not the equal of your employer's wife."

This time his smile was more cheerful. His eyes seemed to tease her, though she could not imagine anything humorous in what she had said. "I shouldn't hazard a wager against you. I saw you handle your brother's team last night."

"Ah," she reminded him quickly, "but think how badly I should handle a frigate at sea! Des has his own abilities."

"I am sure that he has."

She acknowledged this none too enthusiastic praise of her brother and stepped past him, onto the path leading downward toward Queen's Square and the busy heart of the town.

Why had he been so interested in her riding habits? She wondered uneasily if she had given the young groom a rather improper view of herself.

But he remained in her thoughts for some time, despite all her efforts to busy herself with other matters.

When she reached the house in Queen's Square she discovered to her disgust that Des and Colonel Forbin were still in the throes of analyzing the Princess Eulalie's charm and, worse, they had not missed her.

It was a lowering reflection.

Chapter Six

With one hand holding Zephine's reins loosely, Prince Andre watched the young woman move down the pebbled path with her healthy, graceful stride. In those respects young Miss Jasper put him in mind of Zephine. Though a commoner whose dubious antecedents had accumulated their fortune in trade, she carried herself with a pride that could not be exceeded by Eulalie herself. In point of fact, there was more pride and considerably more humor in Miss Hannah Jasper.

The fact that she had not recognized him was of considerable benefit to him. He was used to the toadying efforts of parents with eligible daughters trying to persuade him that these hapless pawns would make ideal wives. Invariably, the young ladies in question were charmed with the idea of acquiring a title high in the ranks of the ancient nobility, but he was never sure that their interest in him was sincere. Miss Jasper, who obviously thought he was a groom, was very much herself, and the result enchanted him. Perhaps it was the novelty of this treatment, but in any case, he found much to admire in her.

Not that a man who had known the enchanting Eulalie's love could ever accept the more earthy Hannah in his heart, but physically, there were attractions. He had often felt that Eulalie's delicacy prevented her from responding to his passions.

On the other hand, the excitement the plebian Hannah aroused in him was undeniable. He wouldn't soon forget the sight of that slender filly hopping around on one beautifully shaped foot a few minutes ago and looking flustered when she saw that she was observed. She might be a commoner and a little inclined to have her own way, due to a complaisant brother, but that could be mended, and she intrigued him far more than any of her rivals in Lady Fiona's painted miniatures.

There was pretty little Clarissa Tremoyle, for one instance. He had heard her name pronounced last night as he removed his coachman's greatcoat and sent Fiona off on that vain errand to request Miss Hannah Jasper as his partner in the country dances. The Tremoyle girl was scarcely out of pinafores. It seemed ludicrous, not to say shocking, to consider her as his bride.

He mounted Zephine and glanced again at the Croft windows. She was there as he had known she would be, with the fingers of one hand pressed against the pane in their special signal. It meant that she was touching his fingertips. He had invented this childish romantic gesture when he was ten and Eulalie seven. She had been crying because they were forced to part, Eulalie being taken to some tiresome French countess living on the edge of gentility in Sussex.

Andre-Charles was going off to win financial support for the emigres who hadn't yet made their peace with the Emperor Napoleon. Even at the age of ten he had despised his task, eternally trying to smile, trying to please, yet being shown such absurd formality, as if he were the Dauphin of France himself. He had been told at the age of eight that the son of Marie Antoinette and Louis XVI was dead. He himself was far, far down the line of succession. During his teenage years when he and Eulalie talked again of marriage and dynasty, it was said that General Bonaparte rescued France from the Terror and its aftermath. This removed Andre-Charles even further away from his "heritage," the wild dreams of his advisers who faded, one by one, through age and death, or simply vanished when the last of the ancestral jewels went into the hands of money-lenders.

Eulalie. The curtains were gently parted and he saw her pale face, imagining it as he knew it to be at close view, the skin almost transparent over the delicate bones, the great blue eyes, the soft mouth, and the nose, which had luckily not inherited the Hapsburg heaviness. He often wondered at her gentleness, for he knew she was not universally liked. Perhaps the very perfection of her manners, whenever they met, was oppressive to less endowed individuals, or perhaps it was her supreme concern for herself. He had always recognized this.

His smile as he looked up at her was forced. The last dream was gone now, or would be, the moment he took his bride for her fortune. Another despicable act in a life he was coming to loathe, a life he owed to a family name that had never been chosen by him. There were moments this morning, and last night before the Assembly Rooms, when he had wished he might remain a "coachman" or a "groom" forever.

"Zephine, go!" he called in the ear of the mettlesome mare. Zephine went, bearing him away from temptation, away from memories of his golden childhood with Eulalie.

A summer breeze fresh with sweet odors of hay and fresh-scythed grass livened the air, brushing his face, giving him a curious kind of hope and optimism. With Everdene Hall looming at the far end of the open drive, and fresh, rolling green in all directions, he wondered if it would ever seem to be his home. Financially, it was far beyond his touch, a fact that did not endear it to him.

Its comforts were modern: a Rumford closed stove in place of the open fireplace, which Lady Fiona assured him would produce miracles of delicious food. She had the cook's word on it. According to her, Sarah Gimmerty was in ecstasies over it. There was Hepplewhite furniture in place of the heavy oak pieces from the Jacobean period, and as much sunlight as could be crowded in through the casement windows. Sash windows had even replaced some of these, and of course, there were long French doors that opened onto the north portico.

He had thought when he ordered purchase of the Hall that it would convince Eulalie he was able to provide an appropriate home for her. Even now it sickened him when he realized he had not made the purchase rapidly enough to prevent Eulalie's appalling marriage. He thanked heaven he had had the sense to reduce his staff drastically. It shocked his few lordly connections from abroad, but at the least, it did not add to his indebtedness.

The big Irish gypsy Meiggs, his gatekeeper, groom, and guardian angel, opened the wrought-iron gates to him and strode up the drive beside Zephine while he played upon a lifetime's acquaintance with the prince to inquire about his morning canter.

"Paid your respects to our fairy tale princess, Sir?"

It was not a subject the prince wanted to discuss. The subject was still a raw wound, even with this old comrade, who had set him on his first mount. He knew he should not have gone by her lodgings in the Crescent this morning, and the mere fact that she had come out to warn him away, reciting the danger if her dreadful boor of a husband caught him, had only made him feel foolish. He could not imagine why he had taken this idiotic ride, and in her direction. Her close proximity made him aware once more of what he had lost.

"She is now Mrs. Samson Croft, you know." He added quietly, hoping Meiggs would accept the hint, "She no longer belongs to us, and we must respect her new life."

"Ay, so we must. Still and all, the old gentleman's well onto the century mark, they do say. And even a tough old hound's got to be put down when he's toothless and lost the scent."

Startled and repulsed by the knowledge that this thought had flitted across his own mind once or twice, the prince said stiffly, "No more. Never let me hear you rambling on in that way again. And he is not a hundred years old but only eighty-five.''

"Only eighty-five, Highness? And yourself a vigorous twenty-nine, if I've me numbers right.''

The prince's mouth set, and Meiggs, who knew all the signs, decided not to tempt fate. He said no more on that head but left His Highness on the steps beneath the gleaming white palladian front of the Hall after wishing him, ''A very good night to yez, Sir. And if ye've ever a mite of a question about a sartain Miss Jasper, ye've only to come by me.''

This gossipy tone came perilously close to an insult against Miss Jasper, and the prince ignored it, though he did not forget it.

The door had opened inward upon the spacious, sunlit entry hall, and His Highness was greeted wordlessly by Abercrombie, the starchy butler whose lean, severe facade belied his one-time task as procurer for Andre-Charles's father, His late Royal Highness. It had been a task that should have put Abercrombie in Lady Fiona's bad books, but the two got on with an ease that surprised the present prince until Lady Fiona explained that in this manner she herself had passed judgment upon all her rivals.

Andre-Charles was soon aware that, as usual, every member of his entourage waited to analyze his mood, hoping by this means to discover which of the candidates for his hand was pulling out into the stretch. Lady Fiona had a knowing look, but even she was forced to confess what all of Bath was gossiping about, that Miss Hannah Jasper had refused to stand up with His Highness at the New Assembly Rooms last night.

The prince was used to being the center of gossip, and it amused him that since he was new to the county many of Bath's good citizens had confused his identity with that of poor, stout, old General Hoogstratten, who had been his father's aide and now served Prince Andre in that capacity as well as confidant and occasional lecturer on the proprieties of royalty.

Lady Fiona must have been on the watch for him in the doorway of the ground floor music room. When she called to him he had already started up the splendid old staircase, whose solemnity was relieved by the sparkle of the freshly washed crystal chandelier dangling above the half-landing. He stopped with one hand on the handrail, wishing for the thousandth time that his well-meaning household would not "hover." There was never any privacy, no hiding-place where he might be alone, without those eternally watchful eyes.

His father, the soul of politeness to his fancy pieces, had a regal disregard for the feelings of his attendants, many of whom served him with little hope of payment beyond the royal smile. Very early in life Prince Andre had winced at the pain inflicted on the staff by his father's indifference and rudeness. He had privately sworn never to behave badly to them, and when he did so upon some provocation, he was heartily sorry. He tried to make it up to the offended party as best he could.

Possibly this explained what he knew at the age of twenty-nine, that they were incredibly loyal to him in spite of the long and often embarrassing delay in the payment of their wages.

"Yes, Fiona?"

The lady rustled up the stairs after him. On the landing she dipped a brief curtsy, barely rising before she suggested with a spark of excitement, "I wonder, shall I visit the Jasper house and intimate that the young lady mistook General Hoogstratten for Your Highness?"

"Thank you, no." He knew others must be listening and understood their curiosity. His future bride would be their new employer, the chatelaine of this household, not the imperious Princess Eulalie, whom they had known all her life, but a commonplace young woman without the least notion of proper conduct in a royal household.

Lady Fiona took a step backward.

"No? But sir . . ."

"At the proper moment." In a sudden burst of frankness he confided, "I am enjoying this role. Andre-Charles of Nowhere, groom and occasional coachman. Furthermore, Fiona, I do believe the young lady has taken a small fancy—a very small fancy—to Andre the Coachman." His features were so much more cheerful she found his mood contagious.

"I am not in the least surprised, Sir. Forgive my frankness, but it is not entirely Your Highness's position that attracts so many candidates in the marriage stakes."

He should have been pleased, but the fact that he was "hanging out for an heiress," as the vulgar wits had it, embarrassed and humiliated him.

"I do not refine upon the motives of young ladies, Fiona." He laughed, touched her jeweled hand briefly. "The female mind is a complicated maze to me. I only hope I may make a reasonably kind husband to the lady who honors me with her hand."

"Of course. But if I should chance upon Miss Jasper in the Pump Room or elsewhere, I thought a hint in the lady's ear might make all smooth for Your Highness."

"I forbid it!"

This sounded so like His Highness's grandfather in a royal rage that every invisible member of the staff within hearing shivered. The luckless Lady Fiona sank into a deep curtsy, murmuring, "As Your Highness commands."

More gently, he went on. "I have your promise?"

She inclined her head. "I swear it, Sir." But she could not help reflecting that this was a household on the sharp edge of poverty, and still His Highness dallied with Miss Jasper, playing groom and coachman while the world tumbled about all their heads. Nor was she reassured some hours later when she heard His Highness order his valet, "Lay by the clothing I wore this morning."

"Will you be riding tonight, Sir?" The young valet was clearly as surprised as Lady Fiona.

"I may be."

It was very odd and quite unlike the prince. Surely His Highness did not intend to play a call in a groom's wretched clothing!

The butler, Abercrombie, who had heard this information, muttered to Lady Fiona, "We are no nearer to a betrothal. Has His Highness run mad? He will not win an heiress while he masquerades as a groom."

But the idea gave Lady Fiona second thoughts.

"I am not so sure. We females take odd humors. And if we are to speak of odd humors, I only hope His Highness has not taken it into his head to pay a call on Princess Eulalie in disguise."

Chapter Seven

Desmond Jasper peered out the front windows down to Queen's Square and sighed loudly, hoping to arouse his sister's interest in his boredom. He achieved nothing with his sighs. Miss Quilling would have given him her gruff sympathy, but she was away in London having a tooth drawn and probably scolding her niece's roistering family of six boys into respectable young adults.

The drumming of his fingers upon the window finally annoyed Hannah sufficiently. She looked up from the mending of sheets—it was a task she loathed, but she had been reared by a careful mother who remembered a childhood in the poverty of a West Yorkshire milling town. Every farthing counted as much as a guinea with Hannah.

"Des, do be easy. You are trying my patience."

"Not a soul out there. Even those endless little females in their pinafores are locked away for the night. It baffles me why Grandfather insisted on building where the place is swarming with seminaries and female academies."

"Because they were not here when Grandpapa built Jasper House," she reminded him reasonably. "Des, why don't you engage a few lively spirits for a card party or something of the sort? Elsewhere."

"It's to no purpose. I've sent around to George Forbin, but he is off to his aunt in Derbyshire. He has expectations in that quarter. And Tom MacInerny and Beau Croft are engaged for a private party at the Croft apartments in the Crescent.''

Hannah remained cynical. This was so like her conniving childhood friend.

"Beau? Mending his fences and his manners? I wouldn't hazard a wager on it.''

"Still,'' Des persisted, "I'd give a hundred guineas to be one of the guests. To meet that incomparable lady again.''

She was perfectly aware that the real object of his interest in the Croft evening party was the princess. Because the subject annoyed her, she teased him. "I am on excellent terms with Mr. Croft. Or at all events, I was so some years ago. Why don't we simply invite the gentleman to an evening of piquet with you, or a general party of cards? He was a consistent winner at faro, Father said.''

"What the deuce would be my interest in Samson Croft?'' he demanded crossly. "The old ogre set his dogs on me once.''

"He'll do worse than set his dogs on you if you behave like a moon-calf over his wife.''

Des colored and would have made a denial, but an unexpected sight in the square below distracted him. He brightened.

"By Gad, we've a visitor! That should relieve this appalling boredom.''

"Thank you.''

"Well, deuce take it, you know what I mean.''

He reached for the bellpull. At this hour of the night, after most plans had been made and before the expected return of the two Jaspers from their evening's entertainment, the servants were caught between their day livery and the night clothes that could be rapidly covered by appropriate robes. Des removed his hand from the bellpull and studied the approaching visitor more closely.

"Why wake the servants for that fellow? What can he want in Queen's Square?''

"Who, in heaven's name?''

He squinted. "There. In the lamplight. That confounded fellow who ran his team into mine at the Upper Rooms last night."

She dropped her sheets and moved to the window.

"It is my impression he was rubbing down his team when your pair came prancing in upon him."

He shrugged and grinned. The front door knocker banged several times. Des grumbled, "I can't think what a coachman is doing, riding a high-stepper up to our door. And at this hour."

"Nor can I."

"What did you say to him last night?"

"I? Not a word amiss, I assure you. He was quite well-spoken, in most respects."

The knocker sounded again. Des went out to the hall above the narrow white and gold staircase and looked over the balustrade. The Jasper butler, an aged valetudinarian, shuffled toward the front door at the same time.

Hannah, coming out into the hall behind her brother, saw the young coachman-groom standing hatless below in a dark greatcoat whose standing collars flattered his olive skin and warm, lively brown eyes. Hannah nudged Des, who called down, "What does the fellow want?"

The young man looked up at them.

"It's me master, Sir. He's given a command, as the saying goes."

"A command?" Des echoed hotly.

"Ay. That'll be the truth on it. His Royal Highness, Prince Andre-Charles-Louis de Bourbon-Valois, will be riding in the morning. May he take up Miss Jasper and her groom at nine? There's me story, if yez'll oblige, Ma'am?"

She wanted to laugh at his absurd dialect. Surely, no man talked so. And it was this that made her suspect the whole thing was a hum. He had asked her this morning where she rode, a clear hint of his interest in accompanying her. She could hardly be seen alone in the company of a groom who was not her own servant, but if her groom accompanied

53

them at a respectful distance, it might be supposed this young man was leading her to his employer.

However, the lie that his employer was the Poverty-Prince needed investigating. Why didn't he tell the truth, that Samson Croft was his master? Or had he been lying to her this morning?

Clearly, he was a born rogue.

Des began haughtily, "My sister does not answer to royal commands." Thinking this over, he amended, "Unless it be Prinny—I mean, our own prince. So take yourself off, my good man."

The audacious young man looked from Des to Hannah, his dark eyebrows gently raised.

"Well now, Mum, 'twon't do to overset His Royal Highness. Mighty high in the instep is our Prince Andre. He was free with his guillotine in the good old days."

Hannah covered her smile, then replied with as much gravity as she could summon up, "I shouldn't wish to have you lose your head on the guillotine, nor mine, when it comes to that. I shall be honored to ride with His Highness tomorrow morning."

The young man bowed and backed out.

Des returned to the Small-Drawing Room with Hannah, still grumbling.

"I thought you despised these foreign princelings hanging out for rich brides."

Hannah very much doubted that the young groom had come from Prince Andre-Charles, et cetera. But then, of course, he may have told her that farago of nonsense this morning to explain his conversation with Eulalie Croft. It was well known that Prince Andre and Princess Eulalie had once been betrothed, and the morals of royalty were said to be lax. In all probability, if this groom was employed in the prince's service, he had been to see Mrs. Croft with a message from his master, and in loyalty to that master, the groom had lied to Hannah.

She determined to reach the bottom of this little mystery,

though she would certainly see that Desmond's groom accompanied her. However intrigued she might be by the mystery and the young man's part in it, she had no intention of shocking the close-knit little world of Bath by being seen alone in the company of a handsome young groom, no matter whom he served.

Still, her sleep was somewhat disordered. Although she could not have admitted it to anyone, especially to Desmond, she had a distinct impression that the young groom's face and form appeared more than once in her dreams.

In the first light of a sunny golden morning she knew she must refuse the prince's "command." Or had it been the young groom's own invitation all the while? He was audacious enough to have contrived the entire affair. Even this was preferable to his master, the prince, who had let it be known to the polite world that he was marrying for a fortune. What wretched little heiress would be sacrificed to him by an ambitious parent?

With all these stern resolutions she was astonished to find herself in her riding habit at nine the next morning and wearing a hat whose white plume added new brightness to her piquant face, with its frame of golden-chestnut hair neatly clubbed below the hat. Luckily, Desmond had already tooled his phaeton to Bristol for a reunion with several old seagoing comrades who had, so to speak, "swallowed the anchor" and scattered inland. She felt that none of her feeble excuses would explain her present behavior. The youngest schoolgirl must know better than to yield to her present shocking intention.

The housekeeper, Mrs. Plackett, rapped on the door of her sitting room, then peered in, her ruddy face glowing.

"Jemie's walking your horse, Ma'am, and here is a card from His Royal Highness, just arrived." She contradicted herself. "What I mean to say, not *Our* Royal Highness. The gentleman from over the way in Boney's country." She presented the card with a curtsy, which Hannah correctly assigned to the card and not to herself.

"Very well. Tell Jemie and the prince's groom I shall be joining them directly."

Hannah took the card. It certainly was that of Prince Andre-Charles-Louis of Bourbon-Valois. She tapped it against her teeth, considering its significance. So the other story had been a lie. The groom really was in the service of Prince Andre, the penniless, hopeful bridegroom.

If this is so, she thought, and I am about to be presented to the prince, then my roguish friend is acting as a marriage broker, and I shall tax him with that.

It would be amusing, though, if she gave the fat, clumsy prince a taste of his own medicine and let him believe, for a brief time, that his titles had won her over.

Having allowed her rogue friend, the prince's groom, to cool his heels walking his royal master's mounts, and perhaps exchange stable gossip with Des's skillful little groom, Jemie, Hannah started down the stairs in a dignified fashion, only to find the prince's groom standing below her where the staircase fanned out gracefully into the somewhat cramped entry hall. He leaned one elbow negligently against the newel post and smiled up at her. He was an impudent fellow, no mistake. She did not return his smile, but her mouth quivered with the effort to retain her dignity.

"You should have remained outside with Jemie," she said at once.

His cheerful misunderstanding was maddening.

"You mean, to walk the mounts? Oh, no. James—er—Jemie does manage tolerably well. Of course, he needs training, but I daresay, in time he will be adequate to his post."

"Adequate!" She accepted the riding crop Kitty thrust into her hand and shook it very nearly in his face. "I took Jemie in training myself. He is the most satisfactory groom of my acquaintance, I assure you."

"Of your acquaintance, Ma'am, I have no doubt," he agreed smoothly.

She realized he was deliberately baiting her and recovered

after a few seconds' hard breathing. Allowing him to escort her out to the street in style, she moved to another matter on which he could have less skill.

"I note that your English has improved since last night. As an actor you are a very fair groom."

He grinned.

"I have played parts when it seemed appropriate to accomplish my ends. By the by, if it please you, I am called Michael Meiggs."

"I cannot imagine why I should either be pleased or otherwise that you have a name."

She began to suspect that he actually had been an actor at some time. During moments such as this, one might almost imagine from his speech that he was a gentleman as well. She added, "You said you play parts to suit your ends. Others may not know what these ends are, I daresay."

"Miss Jasper, you may very well be the first to know."

She had no time to pursue this line. They were out in Queen's Square and save for the ferretlike, friendly face of Jemie, Desmond's groom, plus three fretting horses, there was certainly no sign of His Royal Highness.

In view of the recent conversation Hannah was particularly loud in her praise of Desmond's young groom.

"How well you handle them, Jemie! Thank you."

But she realized at once that her own beautifully mannered "Rob-Roy" stopped fretting when this rogue of a "Michael Meiggs" stepped away from Hannah and went to Rob-Roy's head. Hannah had often been proud of her own hand with animals, so it seemed reasonable to her that she should be impressed by this sight.

To see what his reply would be, she asked casually, "And where may His Highness have gone to?"

He was prepared. "We are to attend him upon the path. I believe he would like to show you the view of his newly purchased estate. There is an excellent view of Everdene Hall beyond the town and above the Bristol Road."

"I am familiar with Everdene Hall. An elegant pile. Very expensive for the upkeep."

"Indeed," he agreed ruefully. "Or so His Highness has confided. But one must keep up appearances. His Highness owes it to his name."

"What nonsense!"

Jemie was moving to help her mount, but "Michael Meiggs" cupped his hands and knelt. She hesitated, then set her neat boot into his palms and was lifted into the saddle of her russet gelding. Jemie looked puzzled but retreated to his own mount, and "Michael Meiggs" swung easily into the saddle of the sleek black mare he called Zephine.

By the time they had crossed Queen's Square and headed up the heights Hannah suggested that it would be quicker if they passed the Royal Crescent and rode in a westerly direction that would bring them out upon the Everdene road. He hesitated, then shrugged and agreed.

They were just cantering along the path that followed the straight side opposite the Crescent, with its excellent view of the city of Bath, when a young woman also out riding headed toward them at a bruising clip.

Hannah recognized her even at a distance as the Princess Eulalie, looking spectacularly beautiful, her golden curls clustering out beneath the brim of her hat, their color all the more vivid against the black of her habit and the pale sky-blue of her hat-plume. The plume matched her eyes, and her smile at the sight of the three riders was dazzling.

The prince's groom had reined up suddenly at sight of her, and Hannah thought he looked a trifle edgy. The princess cried, "But this is beyond anything great. My groom is laid on his back after a trifling fall two days ago, and I have been in despair of finding suitable company in which to ride. Now, here you are, my—"

"Michael Meiggs," said the groom smoothly as he bowed. "Your Highness may do me the honor of remembering it was I who met you yesterday with messages to your husband from my master. May I present Miss Hannah Jasper, Your Royal Highness?''

"Of course, Miss Jasper. How very good of you to be riding by just when I was so hagged over riding alone. I believe your fine, stalwart brother was presented to me at the Upper Rooms two nights gone. Such a splendid specimen of the British male! So gallant. You must tell him how much I appreciated his sympathy.''

Michael Meiggs and Hannah looked at her intently, Hannah surprised that she should mention something that might lead to speculation about her bridegroom's mistreatment.

The princess blushed and caught her lip between her small, even teeth.

"I mean to say . . . I had struck my hand as I . . . as we descended the staircase on our way to the ball that night. So careless of me!''

"How is it now?'' Michael Meiggs asked without prefixing the question with her title. It was so abrupt and expressed so much concern Hannah was puzzled. She knew he was impudent, but this passed all bounds.

The princess was quick to peel off her glove, revealing a nasty discolored bruise over the tender white inner flesh of her wrist.

"Mr. Croft is truly warm-hearted and generous. When I injured myself he very sweetly presented this bauble to me last evening. A wristlet of gold studded with tiny sapphires. So considerate.''

Hannah stared at the blue-black prints on her wrist, above the bracelet. She scarcely saw the "bauble.'' Surely, Des told her that the princess's bruises appeared across her knuckles. This was quite a different bruise. Could it be a new hurt inflicted by Samson Croft?

Michael Meiggs, too, stared at Mrs. Croft's wrist. He looked tense, pale, and angry. He started to say something, then bit it off as the princess covered her wrist hurriedly.

"But where are we to ride, Miss Jasper?'' she asked Hannah, ignoring the two grooms.

59

"We are to meet His Highness, Prince Andre, on a certain promontory where there is an excellent view of his new estates. I am familiar with the point. It is often the scene of summer gatherings."

The princess looked confused. "You are to meet His Highness . . . there?" She recovered rapidly and laughed, a light, happy little trill. "But that is delightful. I would not miss it for worlds. If you've no objection, I should so enjoy meeting His Highness in his proper milieu."

Hannah did not regard a roadside as the proper milieu of a prince, but clearly the princess had some motive in inviting herself to join them in their ride. Probably, she used this excuse to be seen quite respectably in the company of the prince she had loved before her rich marriage, though it was difficult to imagine that a Great Love was encompassed by this beautiful creature and the stout old prince Hannah had seen at the Assembly Rooms.

And I am to play chaperone, she reflected. I and these two grooms. It was a lowering thought. Nor did Michael Meiggs approve of the princess's presence. For some reason he seemed dissatisfied and fell back to Jemie's side, leaving the place beside Hannah to the new Mrs. Croft.

But during the next few minutes Hannah could not acquit the princess of flirting with the fellow. She made many trivial remarks, forever turning to receive the endorsement of Michael Meiggs.

"Is His Highness still of the same mind about his future plans, Michael?"

"Who can say, Ma'am?"

"Is His Highness engaged on Friday week? Mr. Croft and I are giving a waltzing party for a few friends. Will His Highness be accounted one of them?"

"That I cannot say, Ma'am."

The princess continued to plague the groom. "His Highness is such a splendid man, is he not? What times we had in those glorious days when we were very young! Does His Highness ever speak of them? Or of me?"

"Of you, Mrs. Croft?"

"Very true," she acknowledged. "I am now Mrs. Croft. But you may tell him that Mrs. Croft will never forget those days of her youth." Turning to look back at him, she raised her right hand for emphasis, but the gauntlet of her glove had fallen back, and Michael Meiggs could plainly see the bruise on her wrist as well as the bracelet that may have been her husband's gift to salve the wound.

Hannah glanced back in time to surprise an uncommonly somber look on the young groom's face. It seemed clear to her that Michael Meiggs must feel vastly more for the princess than anyone, including his master, had any notion.

And what has all this to do with me? she wondered. Am I to be a candidate for the fat prince's hand so he and the princess can "cluck" over that evil pair, Samson Croft and Hannah Jasper, who stand between them and happiness? She resented this only a little more than she resented the flirtatious Michael Meiggs, who seemed capable of flinging his attentions at every female under thirty.

Of one thing she was certain. She was the last heiress in the kingdom to desire a princely husband.

But she also resented Eulalie Croft's delicate, graceful appearance on horseback. The princess was clearly displaying her abilities for the benefit of Hannah and the two grooms. Hannah moved ahead, saying with an impatient laugh, "Come. Let us have a gallop. We are none so far from that high ground above Everdene Great Park where His Highness is to meet us."

"A race? Dare we?" the princess murmured, with a quick look over her shoulder. "Still," she agreed after an instant, "I am accounted in some quarters to be a tolerable horsewoman. Fortunately, we have left behind those dreadful pebbles, which, I confess, alarm me a trifle, the way they fly about."

Michael Meiggs, who took a great deal upon himself, called, "No. Wait. Another time. And God knows, another place!" He started forward, but the two women were al-

61

ready off at a bracing pace, urged on by a sense of rivalry that Hannah, at least, did not understand.

The path spread out under heavy summer foliage, the sun dappling the ground and the tunnel view ahead through the trees. Hannah, being the taller of the two, leaned far forward with an occasional exhortation to Rob-Roy, "On, boy. There's my brave lad."

Ahead, the height of the trees raised as they came out into wilder country, and Hannah found the princess's mount pulling up neck-and-neck with Rob-Roy.

"The point. Ahead to the right, by that large chestnut tree," Hannah called. She caught glimpses of Eulalie's face and during those seconds was puzzled by an image that appeared to be superimposed over the angelic sweetness of that golden creature. The teeth bared, the eyes narrowed, the muscles hardened, Princess Eulalie was throwing everything into this friendly gallop.

The big chestnut tree loomed up, the only one in this area, a shelter and goal for many supper parties out of Bath. Later in the day a delicious picnic might be laid on the grass under that tree for several young people properly chaperoned, but it was still too early in the day for parties of pleasure. A dead branch extended from the trunk of the tree, far below the bright foliage, and Hannah, who knew it well, ducked her head upon approaching it, but the princess, following her direction, cut in front of her at that moment. This caused Hannah to raise her head quickly in the effort to forestall a collision.

The top of her hat was caught by the branch, and the resulting jolt panicked Rob-Roy who reared up, pitching Hannah to the ground in a flurry of skirts and green leaves shaken loose from the higher branches.

Striking the ground in a bundle, she was momentarily dazed but knew even in this instant that no bones were broken. Only her pride and dignity were badly injured.

While the princess controlled her own mount, all the while uttering cries of distress, apology, and explanation, the two grooms rushed to Hannah's aid, Michael Meiggs turning her over gently and lifting her head so that it was propped on his thigh.

Hannah was within a second of opening her eyes when, in an angry voice she had not yet heard from him, he demanded of the princess, "Why did you do such an asinine thing, Lalie? You are a better rider than that."

Lalie? From a groom addressed to Her Royal Highness?

The answer rushed out in trembling accents from the princess's mouth. "Oh, Andre, I never meant to. She said that tree was our goal. Is she dead? My God, what a scandal!"

So much for the true identity of *Michael Meiggs!*

For a minute or two Hannah lay there motionless on the grass, gathering her wits and eavesdropping on this enlightening dialogue. Throughout these moments, however, one refrain came through to her ever more forcefully.

She had been an addlepated fool to be so easily taken in. Surely, no coachman, no uneducated groom, talked as this one did. He was born a gentleman. She had always suspected it. Her common sense had repeatedly warned her, but she persisted in falling under the spell of this "playactor."

Indeed, he had boasted to her less than an hour ago that he played several parts. His most successful role had certainly been that of coachman-groom, although, she had to confess, his first performance had been accidental. It was her own mistake when she saw him outside the Assembly Rooms and assumed because she had not seen his evening clothes beneath that coachman's greatcoat that he must be what the coat proclaimed him.

Hannah heard the princess dismount and kneel carefully beside Prince Andre. Her perfume was heavy upon the air. "At all events, she is breathing. We must be grateful for that. Andre, why did she do such a thing? So careless of her! She drew rein so sharply I could not avoid her."

Hannah bristled within but tried to keep her body from betraying her rage.

The prince said at once, "I saw you, Lalie. You forget, I know how impetuous you are."

"My darling, you don't know me at all. I take great care. You cannot believe I married Mr. Croft without long searching of my heart. I knew that as Mr. Croft's wife I should be in a position to help you in many ways. Financially, of course. But in other ways."

"I do not need your help financially, or otherwise."

"If you mean to sacrifice yourself for a fortune . . ."

But he was busy over Hannah. One hand moved across her face. He removed her hat, which had been pushed to the back of her head, and felt carefully over the back of her skull, beneath her disheveled hair, apparently searching for a head wound. Hannah steeled herself against the prickling excitement of his touch. What a rogue he was! A scoundrel in despite of his fine title.

Beyond anything was the knowledge that each trick this fine and noble prince had performed in her presence was toward one end, to pay for lavish estates like Everdene and his own grand, princely life, with Grandfather Jasper's hard-earned fortune. Most probably, he also meant to retain Mrs. Croft's regard.

Prince Andre-Charles-et-cetera deserved—she did not know what dreadful fate, and she meant to pay him out.

Chapter Eight

Prince Andre caressed Miss Jasper's soft, tangled hair with an unaccustomed concern.

His life and his position had given him a choice of numerous mistresses of surprisingly high station among the *haut ton* of the Regent's circle, but his youthful love for the Princess Eulalie had remained a constant, a matter made subtly known to his various mistresses. These ladies, in their turn, enjoyed his attentions but showed no signs of heartbreak when the affair ended. They understood the rules of the game.

Prince Andre felt fairly sure that Miss Hannah Jasper was not of that stripe, and for some incomprehensible reason, he found himself pleased that this was so.

As a result, he felt a special tenderness toward her, and the shock of seeing her unceremoniously tilted off Rob-Roy's back and dropped onto the grass had jolted him hard.

He did not question the fact that it was Eulalie's fault. He had seldom known Eulalie to be so clumsy. She was an accomplished horsewoman in spite of her fragile appearance. But he laid her clumsiness to the fact that so much had happened to her of late. The second bruise, this time on her wrist, was the outside of enough. For one blinding second when she revealed it to him, so unconsciously, and then loyally lied about it, he had felt a killing rage toward Samson Croft.

Yes. She could not be held accountable for the accident to Miss Jasper. It was all the fault of Samson Croft. Without actually telling him of her husband's brutality in so many words yesterday morning, Eulalie had tacitly admitted her husband's vile temper. The rest, the brutal marks on her knuckles and then on her wrist, were obviously the results of that brutality.

Her talk of Samson Croft's "gift," the wristlet, told him that this was her husband's bribe to erase memories of his cruelty. And yet how quickly and loyally Eulalie had lied to save her husband from universal abhorrence! Small wonder that her riding had suffered this morning. He only wished her problems had not caused Hannah to suffer as well.

Hannah shifted her head and groaned. It was an artistic sound, but the prince was much too concerned to notice the level of her performance. He murmured with relief, "Ah, that is more like it. How are you feeling, Miss Jasper?"

She opened her eyes, her long lashes fluttering. They were extraordinarily expressive, but he found himself worried again by the steady regard of her large hazel eyes.

"You can see me, Miss Jasper, I trust."

She murmured softly, "Oh, yes. I am only a little shaken. If I might have your strong arm, I am persuaded I should be able to stand."

"Are you sure?"

"Quite."

He was a trifle cross with Eulalie, who interposed impatiently, "You see? She is very much herself. You will do splendidly, Miss Jasper, won't you? She can stand. All is well. Let her go. She will manage."

He was crisp and direct. "Nonsense. She is trembling. I will carry her. Miss Jasper, we are near to Everdene Great Park. Let me take you there."

"I couldn't. His Highness would take it very ill. You note that he was not here to meet us. He is angry with me. I refused when he commanded me to stand up with him at the Upper Rooms the other night."

"Not commanded, surely," he teased. "He is not at all the sort to puff up his own consequence, I assure you."

She blinked, her slim fingers curving around his. "Oh, no. I am quite in awe of him. But if you think it proper, perhaps I might feel more the thing after a glass of ratafia. Or whatever His Highness's cellars may have to revive one."

He was pleased. Thank God she was not too missish to accept his invitation or even to accept a reviving glass of something stronger, of which she was plainly in need. She looked pale, and her form was a mere nothing in his arms as he supported her. She made a small effort to free herself, but it was clear to him that the strength to walk was beyond her at the moment. He called to the anxious Jasper groom, who gave over the reins of Eulalie's horse and shuffled forward with his own and Miss Jasper's mounts.

"How is Miss? She be lookin' purely white. That'll be none so good."

"She is in fine fettle. She will be very much herself in no time. You must escort Mrs. Croft to the Crescent. I will carry Miss Jasper back to Queen's Square in my curricle, once she has rested."

"What? Jemie Cade to be going aside of a princess? Lor', wait'll I tell 'em down to the stables."

The princess laughed. "We shall deal well together, Jemie Cade."

Prince Andre watched her bestow upon the dazzled boy her look with which he was so familiar, a look that told the recipient he was her sole concern in all the world. But Jemie owed his first loyalty to Miss Jasper and he asked hesitantly, "You'll be takin' her up in your curricle, Sir?"

Obviously, he had heard the first brief words between Prince Andre and the princess. "Yes, yes. Do not concern yourself. Please give Miss Jasper your arm while I mount. Then I will take her."

Eulalie was already mounted. From long sensitivity to her presence and its magical effect, Prince Andre knew her blue eyes were fixed upon him now, willing him to look at her.

Despite a certain revulsion at obeying her enchanting but willful tricks, he found himself returning her stare. As always, she excited him. There was much of the enchantress about Eulalie. It was as if in seeing her he relived their youth, their golden hopes of a future together.

She extended her hand. He took it in his and touched her fingers with his lips.

"Another day, a longer ride, Your Highness? Perhaps Mr. Croft will join you."

"Very likely. And do not fail to express my very good wishes to your master." She glanced at Miss Jasper, who was in the charge of the Jasper groom. "Farewell, Meiggs—that was your name?" she added with her teasing little smile.

"Michael Meiggs, Your Highness."

She was gone. The world of summer under the chestnut tree lost a little of its brightness. He mounted Zephine and extended his arms. Hannah Jasper seemed flustered and a little embarrassed, but with her groom's help, Prince Andre lifted her before him on Zephine's back.

She protested, "Your poor mare! This is ill-judged."

"Zephine is up to our weight, I assure you. Hold tight to my neck and my waist. Ah! Are you quite comfortable?"

She giggled. The sound was endearing, and he suspected her embarrassment came from the fact that she found herself shockingly close in the arms of a groom. The bourgeois classes observed rigid rules about such things. Knowing this, he had been fully aware of her confusion when she was accosted by him and forced to see him as neither a groom nor a prince but a man. It had long been his ambition to discover his real worth without the ancestral trappings. He was delighted that chance had permitted this independent yet vulnerable young lady to be the first to know Andre-Charles-Louis de Bourbon-Valois as himself. Or rather, as Michael Meiggs.

But very soon she must learn the truth. More especially when the real Meiggs greeted them as they passed the gates of Everdene Hall and the Great Park. He laughed silently at her astonishment when she should discover the truth. If Hannah Jasper was typical of all the young British ladies of his acquaintance, she would be awed and impressed by his true identity, but being Hannah, she must also retain the stubborn pride that was a part of her charm.

He liked that. She was utterly different from his lost Eulalie, but he could not bear to marry a woman who seemed to be a mirror image of Eulalie and would naturally disappoint him because the soul was not the same.

"Why didn't he wait for us?" Miss Jasper asked.

He held her body before him, between the reins, and found her warm, slight form very pleasant against his.

"Who?"

She stared back at him, surprised. "But His Royal Highness, of course. He was to have met us at the chestnut tree, you said."

Now was the moment for confession, but he was enjoying his present identity too much. He hesitated, and the moment was lost. His excuse sounded lame, even in his own ears.

"His Highness is very changeful."

"Detestable creature."

He was shaken by that. "Do you find him so?"

"How do I know?" she asked crossly. "I have never met the fellow."

He was troubled again. "I would say he is a fair master, as princes go. They are born under severe handicaps."

"Truly? I should never have thought so." Her innocent gaze held him. "How?"

"H-how?"

"Yes. How are they handicapped?" Still on that note of wide-eyed interest, before he could reply she added, "They are born to believe that entire populations owe them loyalty, devotion, not to mention their lives." She added as an afterthought, "And their fortunes."

The trend of this conversation was not pleasant. He had never dreamed that the sycophants who pursued him from his earliest days might harbor deep resentments against their prince.

The prince softened his quick defense, turning the matter to a jest.

"I am persuaded His Royal Highness will be a better man for the reminder."

"You will remind him? You take a great deal upon yourself—for a groom."

"Well, we are old friends. Indeed, I may say I have known His Highness since time out of mind. He will listen to me."

They had reached a point where the path crossed both the Bristol High Road and the smaller, less traveled road to Everdene Hall. Thanks to the rolling open countryside of the Great Park, the Hall stood out on a slight knoll about a mile away. One of the big iron gates of the estate stood open, which meant that the real Meiggs expected the prince to return at any minute.

If the prince's luck held he might not have to summon Meiggs by name and could continue the masquerade a few minutes longer. To what purpose he did not know. His true identity must be revealed sooner or later. He had become more and more uneasy over the unmasking, and he laid this to Miss Jasper's evident dislike of royalty.

But with every meeting he had become more determined that Hannah Jasper should be the leading candidate for his wife. Since Eulalie was as far beyond his reach as the sun, he would make the best of things with the moonlight, and Hannah Jasper. An admirable second choice. He considered himself lucky to have first encountered her in that unorthodox way outside the Assembly Rooms. He saw a piquant, challenging, even tantalizing young lady whom he might never have discovered if he had first become known to her as His Royal Highness.

The big gypsy, Meiggs, came down the straight gravel drive to the gates, waving to the prince, who called to him quickly as Zephine passed between the gates.

"We shall be leaving again shortly." And with emphasis, "I did not encounter His Highness. He must have had a change of mind."

"Indeed, Your . . . Indeed," Meiggs stammered, understanding very little. "As you say."

Zephine cantered along the straight drive while the prince grinned, well aware of the confusion he had left behind him.

Meiggs pulled the gates ajar and loped along after Zephine. There should have been more danger of exposure at the Hall, but by great good fortune, after the prince had let Hannah slip easily through his hands into Meiggs's powerful arms, Lady Fiona Westerby arrived on the scene, together with the butler and a footman. Lady Fiona was a woman of quick wits.

The prince addressed her directly.

"His Highness did not meet us, but Miss Jasper had a fall. She is recovered now, but I think a drop of reviving brandy would not go amiss. I feel sure His Highness would approve."

Lady Fiona caught herself in the beginnings of a curtsy, rose and said, "Certainly. Are you able to walk, Miss Jasper? How very nice to see you! I am an old friend of your good brother's, you know. We met at Carlton House. One of Prinny's London affairs. Captain Desmond gallantly rescued me from a dreadful crush."

Miss Jasper seemed to be much more herself, the prince saw, to his great relief. She walked up the steps, ignoring Meiggs and the others, and saying to Lady Fiona on a note of ironic humor, "It is my brother's role in life, I believe, the rescue of lovely ladies."

The prince suspected that poor Lady Fiona would like to consider her own "rescue" a special circumstance in Sir Desmond's life, but Miss Jasper had neatly scotched that. Lady Fiona raised her voice; for Prince Andre's benefit, he made no doubt.

"I wonder. Will Miss Jasper be comfortable in the Ladies' withdrawing room on this floor?"

"A large, cold salon," the prince called. "Very likely, His Highness would wish Miss Jasper to be more comfortable up in the small gold parlor."

The lovely white and gold parlor had been decorated especially for his future bride, the Princess Eulalie, but now that he determined to choose Hannah Jasper as his wife, he wanted to see her in that charming room. He must grow used to another face and figure, not that golden, fairy tale princess with the sun shining in her hair and her fragile fingers caressing his face.

There was also another reason for choosing that salon. Above the mantel were hung small gold-framed portraits of Eulalie and Andre-Charles. He wanted Hannah to see the portrait of himself in his "regalia" before she guessed who he was. That would break to her the news of his true identity.

He was prepared for her quick, spirited anger. But he knew the world and did not doubt her ultimate pleasure over the discovery that she would become a princess, after the requisite training and, unfortunately, a radical change in all her easy manners. It seemed a pity to change anything about Hannah Jasper, but he resigned himself to the fact that it would be necessary.

If Miss Jasper remained romantic—and what young lady of her charm was not?—she would be impressed when he became the prince almost before her eyes.

He watched Lady Fiona go upstairs into the small parlor with Miss Jasper, whom she seated before the cold fireplace before discovering the two portraits over the mantel. Upon seeing the portrait and Andre-Charles's dark eyes gazing down at her, Lady Fiona gave a nervous start and looked quickly at the doorway. The prince nodded. She frowned her puzzlement but made no effort to conceal the portrait.

He hurried down the hall to his own bedchamber and dressing room, where his good-looking young valet, a French emigre named DeVal, was trying to pit his polite insistence against General Hoogstratten's hulking presence.

"Must be here, my lad. Know His Highness would be the first to welcome me. Come, come. No hedging."

The prince stepped into the room. "I am here, Hoog. Did we have an engagement? It seems to have slipped my mind."

"Not at all, dear boy. Merely thought you might be wondering what had become of me. Been riding over the estate, making a survey, you might say. Splendid stuff, the estate. Might even call it a bargain."

The prince did not wish to offend his old friend and companion, but the general was very much in the way, and Prince Andre had little time to change. He clapped the general's broad back and urged him toward the door.

"Perhaps later. I promise you, Hoog, your favorite port. The ghastly sweet stuff you and Father stole from Soult's Frenchies."

"Excellent. I'll hold you to your word, my boy."

The instant the good general waddled out into the upper hall, Andre turned to his valet. "DeVal, can you refurbish me in a matter of minutes?"

"Refurbish, Monseigneur?"

"Make me a prince again, as quickly as possible."

The valet considered. "Eh, bien, the pantaloons go on. The breeches off. The dusty boots off. A few decorations, a tunic of appropriate cut."

He suited the action to the words without once expressing his questions by a single glance. He was a young man of great discretion.

In a matter of minutes the audacious groom had been transformed into Prince Andre-Charles-Louis de Bourbon-Valois, complete with the decorations he seldom wore, and the medals he had not—alas—earned.

"An unexpected engagement, Highness?" DeVal asked casually, removing an invisible thread from the gold braid on one shoulder of Andre's white uniform.

"Expected, I should think. By this time, at all events, since she will have seen the portrait. But I must look my best. She is a lady of strong principles and a dislike of poppinjay princes."

Having discovered the portrait and the identity of her friend the groom, she would know why he had played the trick upon her. Perhaps a brief anger . . . but afterward, her playful humor must overcome her childish prejudice and all would be well.

He studied his reflection in the long oval glass that had belonged to his mother, and was reasonably satisfied. He was no coxcomb, but considering the low degree of even the most ordinary good looks among the present princes of Europe, he felt that Miss Hannah Jasper must admit he was not the worst of the lot.

"Well, on with the yoke," he called to the valet, mimicking a lancer charge.

"The yoke, Monseigneur?"

"The marriage yoke, DeVal. The greatest bondage of all."

He left the young valet staring after him uneasily.

He heard the voice of Lady Fiona before he reached the small parlor. The door had been left ajar by the young footman-in-training who, in the interests of economy, sometimes carried trays at odd hours. The two ladies were sipping Madeira, which seemed to have been Miss Jasper's choice.

Prince Andre made no doubt that when Hannah Jasper discovered from his portrait that she had been tricked, her first reaction would be pique, even a brief burst of anger at having been fooled. He hoped that during the minutes he had been gone she had sufficiently recovered to tease him now, or at least return to that friendly independence he had always found so captivating about her.

Instead, it was he who received a shock very like cold water in the face when he heard her reply to Lady Fiona's nervous plea. "Oh, but all in jest, you know. His Highness has a rare and charming humor."

"That's as may be," his prospective bride said coldly. No, not coldly. Much worse. She said it and all that followed *indifferently*, adding, "The truth is, he made a far more attractive groom than a Prince of the Blood. I fear such creatures hold no interest for me. Such wasted lives, their general lack of intelligence . . .''

''My dear Miss Jasper, forgive me, but you talk like a . . . a Jacobin. One of those dreadful persons across the water who guillotined His Highness's relations. I assure you, His Royal Highness has a very tolerable understanding. He is far from cruel to those who minister to him. And he has no more libertine propensities than the general run of his peers.''

Prince Andre winced at that and was scarcely surprised when Miss Jasper shared his distaste. ''Such faults as may be excusable in a groom are intolerable in a prince. At all events, I fear the subject of royalty has never interested me.'' She set her glass on the table beside her chair, arose, and began to ease her gloves on over those fingers Prince Andre had admired earlier when she lay in his arms. ''I must be returning home. Jemie will have alarmed the household over my fall. If I may borrow one of His Highness's mounts, and perhaps a groom,'' she added with just the right cutting edge, ''one whose credentials are unexceptionable.''

The prince had heard enough insults to lower his self-worth by several degrees. Feeling a complete fool, he managed as much dignity as he could muster and softened this with his smile.

''Surely, Miss Jasper, you will give me one more chance to prove my worth—as a groom.''

''In that livery?'' She indicated his white tunic, with its embarrassing display of ancestral glory that time had long since made irrelevant to the nineteenth century.

He reddened, silently cursing the impulse that made made him imagine she would succumb to such trappings.

''I beg your pardon, Miss Jasper. If you will give me ten minutes, I promise you the groom you called Michael Meiggs will be very much at your service.''

He did not wait for her answer but turned and strode down the lengthy hall to his private quarters. DeVal was still clearing away the dusty and grass-stained signs of his former role when he returned.

"We are not done with the groom yet, DeVal. Help me."

But when he came back to Miss Jasper he met only Lady Fiona, who ran breathlessly up the wide front staircase to meet him on the upper floor.

"Gone, Your Highness. I did my best. I even seized the bridle, but she was too quick for me."

"Bridle? What horse did she take?"

"Zephine was blown, so she took the old black that Meiggs rides. He tried to stop her, but that young lady is something of an autocrat herself. And he says he understood the young lady was leaving at once, in any case. He thought you wanted her to take the horse."

"And he did not attend her?" Prince Andre swore. Lady Fiona stared at him.

"Your Highness?"

"I can't let her leave unescorted. And Zephine is out of the question. It must be one of the others. Where is Meiggs? Meiggs!"

From the wide steps Lady Fiona watched him race across the drive toward the stables and shook her head. General Hoogstratten's heavy tread aroused her to his presence.

"Seems in a devilish hurry."

"His future hangs upon his success in stopping that young lady. Our future as well, General."

"The heiress giving him trouble, is she? But she'll come to hand. Never knew a commoner yet who could resist a title."

"I wonder," Lady Fiona murmured. "She did not seem to be in the common way."

Chapter Nine

Hannah knew almost the exact moment the prince was on her trail. The black gelding hack supported her well, though Meiggs (the *real* Meiggs!) had been reluctant to throw a woman's saddle upon his back, and she had gotten nearly to the Chestnut Tree, with its painful memories, when she realized that the lying, conniving prince had come after her.

How desperately he needed her fortune, arraying himself in that white French tunic, which he must know presented such a breathtakingly handsome creature at his best! Wanting to overwhelm her with his physical attractions, was he? Well, he would catch cold at that game.

She was an excellent rider, with a firm hand, and her mount soon became accustomed to her skirts, but she was forced to slow her pace when they reached the path, with its pebbles and rocks. Even so, the gravel flew in all directions for a minute or two before she brought the black gelding back to a moderate pace. Just as the path mounted the hill and she saw the pale gold Bath stone of the Crescent elipse loom up against a piercingly blue sky, she looked over her shoulder and saw that Prince Andre was within sight behind her.

She certainly did not fear him, but she wanted to give him no opportunity for one of his impudent performances. They were far too persuasive, and it was with relief that she saw Beau Croft riding toward her, away from the Crescent. She waved to him and he made haste to join her, leaning across the space between their mounts to take her hand and kiss the air an inch above the flesh revealed when he turned her gauntlet back.

Hannah's spirits lightened, perhaps under the influence of his euphoric mood.

"You seem to be feeling more the thing than you were at the Upper Rooms. Has your luck improved?"

He grinned, but his eyes narrowed. "You are asking if your guineas are safe. I may happily say they are. I was about to pay a visit in Queen's Square this very morning to demonstrate. Behold!"

She looked down, thunderstruck as he pushed a tiny cloth bag into her palm. No paper here. She felt at once that it was full of coins. These proved to be golden guineas. She could scarcely believe it.

"Beau! Have you turned to the highways to make your fortune?"

"Would you care?"

"Very much. I find the climate around a public gibbet hostile to my tastes."

"Well, you may sleep peaceably of nights, Hannah. The money is honestly earned."

She did not ask how this had occurred, but her glance back at the Crescent was eloquent. Beau Croft shrugged.

"My grandfather has moments of family feeling. It would have been worth the loss to have called him on that ignominious 'Bew' that he persists in calling me."

She laughed. Of course, he had been christened 'Beaufort,'' which would be pronounced in his grandfather's way, but his wide acquaintance saw him as a follower of the better-known Mr. Brummell, and he fostered the idea. To Hannah he had always been Beau.

"So you have made your peace with the lady you profess to dislike so much. Does Mrs. Croft treat you in true maternal fashion? Or should I say—'grandmaternal' ?"

Though they were cantering down into town amid several

chair-boys and two or three street peddlers, any of whom might have overheard him, he said loudly, "She is an ill-used lady, whether she may be my new grandmother or a Bavarian princess."

Hannah stared at him, puzzled by his about-face. Clearly, some influence had been at work. Beau was much too selfish to be moved by another's pain, unless he could profit by interceding, and it baffled her to know how Beau might profit by this sudden attack upon his grandfather. Unless the guineas he was so free with came from Eulalie Croft.

But why? Was it perhaps his personal charm?

The princess could hardly have succumbed to Beau Croft and his rather unconventional qualities so soon after sacrificing the far greater attractions of Prince Andre-Charles.

However much Hannah resented being used by the prince and pursued solely for her fortune, she admitted to herself that he was the most physically prepossessing man she had ever met.

Beau returned her stare with one every bit as suspicious. "Her Highness tells me that the fortune-hunting prince has been pursuing you, with what object you can imagine."

"I can well imagine," she agreed more lightly than she felt. "His object was also that of your new grandmama."

"Very true." He surprised her by the curious streak of frankness that occasionally overset his ruthless and often dishonest habits. "And I have your princeling's own interest in you. Always remember the difference, though. I loved you before a fortune meant anything to me."

"I know." She reached for his hand. He took hers, and they rode on with hands clasped, in excellent charity with each other. Memories of pleasant Northcountry adventures together as children had cemented a relationship that even his taking habits and her sharp way with money hadn't yet destroyed.

It was not until they reached the Jasper House and an anxious Jemie Cade walking up and down over the cobblestones that Hannah was able to see just how nearly the determined, penniless prince had stopped her. He rode down from the heights and reined in his horse across the square and sat there staring at her. She gave him an indignant returning stare, but he spoiled her effort by smiling and inclining his head, still seated on the restive bay mare.

"As though we were still friends," she muttered. Both Beau and Jemie Cade looked surprised as they handed her down from Michael Meigg's horse, and she said brusquely, "The bay belongs to His Highness. Please return it . . . across the square."

Beau glanced across the square, bowed politely to the prince, and laughed.

"She's right, by Gad! There's the fellow. Clearly didn't trust you with his wretched hack. Followed you all the way to fetch it home."

"No doubt."

She turned over the reins to Jemie and started into the house, but couldn't resist looking back once more until Jemie met the prince across the square and offered him the reins. Prince Andre studied the reins as if he had never seen them before, then took them, offered Jemie some small coins, and swung around, heading back up the hill. He did not glance again in Hannah's direction.

She sighed. Beau and the Jaspers' Mrs. Plackett held the door open for her. Beau teased her on a joking note with a sharp edge.

"Regretting you won't become Princess Hannah?"

"You are talking a great deal of nonsense. Will you please be on your way? Unless you want to accompany George Forbin and me to the Pump Room."

Beau looked as though he would object, but she remained cold, and to her relief he left her soon after, complaining that the Pump Room was good for nothing but the aged Bath quizzes.

An hour later, when she and Colonel Forbin walked over to the Pump Room, that rendezvous for all valetudinarians and claimants to the *haut ton* of Bath society, they were just in time to see Samson Croft limp out of a sedan chair in the Abbey Churchyard and approach the Pump Room, leaning heavily on the shoulders of two sturdy chair-boys.

The sight of his leonine head reminded her of his cruelty toward his delicate bride. She was still curious about that and about his true nature. She increased her pace, causing the colonel to forget what he was saying and to stride along beside her, playing the solicitous admirer again.

"Take care, Miss Jasper. Mind the cobbles. I saw a lady trip and fall some days ago."

Hannah cut in upon this boring and, to Hannah, insulting advice. "Why the deuce does he visit the Pump Room without Mrs. Croft? Surely she gives some thought to her husband's ailments."

"Well, she is a princess, despite Old Samson. I have found her all condescension, a delightful young woman. But I daresay, ladies in her position feel that the average visitor to the Baths or the Pump Room is not quite . . ."

"George, you are the soul of tact—Ah, Mr. Samson Croft! I'll wager you do not remember me. Your neighbor in the West Riding when we were both young."

The leonine old head turned. The fierce gray eyes glared out at her from beneath overhanging gray eyebrows.

"There's no neighbor of mine like to greet me with that one but that they're wanting something."

She laughed. As usual when she behaved with the slightest degree of originality, several witnesses, mostly female, were staring at her. The traffic in sedan-chairs, or those Pump Room visitors crossing over from a visit to the ancient Abbey, was now at an absolute stand.

"Mr. Croft, why should I want something of you? Unless it be another slice of that splendid *moogin* you gave me long ago."

The old man's eyebrows came down. Very slowly, his rugged, seamed face broke into a reluctant grin. His voice had not lost its gruffness, but she knew that memories had softened him.

"So ye be that one, luv? Ay. Ye've the bold look of her. Ye're not afeard of Old Samson. Come. Fetch me up a mug of that vile stuff they call 'the waters.' " He grinned then. "If ye please, that is."

"I'll do it, and gladly. To pay you back for the *moogin*, Sir."

"Fair's fair."

He shook off his bearers and put considerable weight on her shoulder. They walked on together with Colonel Forbin following, uncomfortably aware that he had been replaced by an ancient being popularly referred to as "the Ogre."

The long, high-ceilinged, austerely elegant Pump Room, with its ornamental Corinthian columns, was somewhat overcrowded, but this had never troubled Samson Croft. He paid little attention to the strollers, of whom there were dozens, wandering past the fountain at one side of the room, chattering so loudly the little pleasant orchestra was quite drowned out, but when he saw a delicate young gentleman occupying one of the few chairs and flirting with a stout lady somewhat older, he raised his cane and jabbed at the young man unmercifully.

"Out on ye. Stand up like a man and give 'way there to yer betters."

The young man shrank from him, or from the cane, which left the chair undisputedly in Samson Croft's possession. He eased himself down. Hannah did not have the heart to scold him, since it was clear that he was in pain, probably from rheumatism and certainly from gout.

"I'll fetch you a cup of that loathsome water, Mr. Croft, and you must drink every drop."

He said "bah!" but looked as though he expected her to do that very thing.

She made her way through the usual group gossiping around the fountain, greeted several old acquaintances, and was given a cup of the mineral water, which she brought to the old ogre. Making horrid faces, he gulped the vile-tasting stuff while quizzing her.

"What may a pretty young thing like 'e be a-doing in this place? Look about. Never a creetur but is nigh me own age. Not but what I be strong as a bull."

Colonel Forbin felt duty-bound to interrupt this tête-à-tête. "Miss Jasper is here to meet her many friends, Sir. I may say, the certainty of her presence here is precisely what brings the rest of us to this place."

"Really, George," Hannah told him repressively, "you are too absurd. Many people do not agree with you. Mrs. Croft, for example."

"Ay." Samson Croft looked up from his cup. "Ye'll not catch me sweet princess waiting on this young 'un. Don't think half well of us from the North, she don't. But it's no matter. Like a fresh young mare, she'll be brought to the saddle."

Forbin persisted. "But the Princess Eulalie is not a mare, Sir. She is a fragile creature of quite superior blood lines. I trust that she is being treated with special care."

"Certain-sure. What d'ye take me for?"

Hannah thought the colonel was going rather too fast and too far. She herself shared his curiosity but did not like his accusatory tone. She motioned him away. He hesitated, hurt by her anxiety to be rid of him, but a meaning frown from her made him back away reluctantly. He was joined by a young lady and her mother, who immediately engaged him in conversation.

The old man eyed Hannah knowingly.

"Ye've got it on the tip of the tongue to ask me some'ut about my princess. Ask."

"She is truly fragile, Sir. I wondered if you realize that even a firm touch might bruise her."

"Here. Take the cup, if ye please." While she took the cup he stated, "There's one bit of news that will surprise them as knows my princess. She's that clumsy ye'd not credit it."

"Clumsy!" He was right. She could not credit it.

"Come as nigh to a plunge down our main staircase as

makes no matter. Caught her quick as ye may wink. I'm still a spry one.''

Hannah thought of Princess Eulalie's injuries, one to her wrist and one to the knuckles of her right hand. She suggested on a casual note, "And you snatched her back by the wrist?''

He looked at her, his eyebrows stiff and fierce. "Devil a'doubt ye're a mind-reader! 'Twas exactly so.''

"You were a hero, in fact.''

"Eh? Well, I'd not go so far. Accidents happen. Poor lass. She was that shook—you'd scare credit how shook she was.''

"Oh, but indeed, I would!'' She returned to the fountain, setting down the empty cup a second before a full cup of the medicinal water was fitted between her thumb and forefinger. Since this was often the work of a friend or a male presuming on an acquaintance at the New Assembly's Ballroom, she turned to smile and thank him.

She was a good deal shocked to see Prince Andre-Charles, who had just withdrawn his hand. He managed to look the gentleman, but only just, with a riding coat over his groom's breeches and jerkin. Confident and full of charm, he returned her smile just as though she had never parted from him in a flurry of indignation a couple of hours before. She sobered at once. Something in his eyes reminded her that his sense of humor was still very much in play.

She pushed the cup into his hands with unnecessary vigor. "I never take the waters.''

Before he could be properly crushed, as any gentleman would have been, the Dowager Duchess of Buccleigh inserted her ponderous bulk between the prince and Hannah. Her shelflike bosom insinuated itself against the cup in his hand.

"How excessively diverting, to find Your Royal Highness here in the Pump Room! So very gracious. You are all condescension.''

"Your Grace is too kind." He was his usual good-mannered self, though his gaze returned to Hannah with what she might have called flattering interest.

The duchess, who had clearly assumed the cup in his hand was offered to her, accepted it. The prince winced and looked over her shoulder at Hannah, who smiled mischievously and turned away. For an instant it appeared that he would follow her across the room but was prevented by the duchess, who pushed her granddaughter between them. The child curtsied with trembling knees, and the prince gave her his hand, helping her to rise. He started to speak.

The girl stammered at the same time, and her grandmother came to the rescue, booming on in her characteristic voice, "Thank His Royal Highness, my dear. He has fetched you this strengthening cup."

The girl stammered again, then put the cup to her lips, her teeth chattering nervously against the edge of the cup. His Highness glanced Hannah's way, a mere flash, but it made her laugh in spite of herself.

As she replied absently to the colonel's rambling remarks, it occurred to her that her life would be very much more prosaic without the activities of the impudent, princely "groom." It was a pity the game couldn't have continued a little longer, but on her terms.

She might even let him imagine she was determined to be a princess. Let him make his plans. Let his noble retainers do their work. He would grow more and more confident, more and more charming, and in the end he must find that the woman he wished to marry for her fortune did not think him worth the purchase.

The next time His Highness looked her way she would soften her smile and be rewarded by the bright expectation in his romantic eyes.

Full of thoughts of golden guineas, she made no doubt.

Chapter Ten

Hannah was well aware of her brother's weakness for young ladies in distress. Evidence meant little, especially that produced by more level heads with less romantic hearts than his. She knew that her suspicion as to the true cause of Mrs. Samson Croft's injuries would not be enough to move Desmond from his fixed idea: the princess was being ill treated by a devilish cruel husband. Indeed, a new bridegroom!

"It does not bear thinking of," he reiterated for what seemed like the dozenth time since his return home from Bristol. But he continued to think of it and, worse, to speak of it.

Her efforts to calm these all too familiar signs of future trouble were just as vain as she had feared they would be. "Des, I do think you might be reasonable for once in your life. The lady tripped on a flight of stairs and Mr. Croft caught her. That is how she received those marks on her wrist."

He stopped pacing to stare at her incredulously. "You must think me a great gull to believe such a story. How came you to hear it?"

"Samson Croft told me himself."

With the air of one delivering a leveler that would bring her to her knees, he asked, "If this is so, will you have the goodness to explain to me why Her Highness did not see fit to describe this noble deed to her friends? There is no shame attached to relating the so-called heroism of her husband.''

Not being at all sure why the princess played her sinister little game (if, indeed, old Samson spoke the truth), Hannah could only say,

''No doubt, she has her reasons. I should like very much to know what they are.''

''And so should I, for they are not true. The whole thing is a bit of humbug spread by the old ogre to explain his brutality.'' He finished with the unalterable argument, ''I do not forget it was he, after all, who set his dogs on me.''

''You were where you should not have been, Des. You know how fierce those folk in the West Riding are when protecting their property. Why do you think they have those stone walls everywhere? And when Mr. Croft tried to make amends by offering us the gingerbread, you were afraid to eat it.''

''Afraid? You must be mad! I had too much pride to eat the brute's leavings. That was the sum and substance of it.''

Nevertheless, she hoped her words had made some impression upon him. Since he said no more about the sufferings of the new young Mrs. Croft, Hannah could only trust that the matter would fade away when the Crofts returned to their estate in the North. She devoutly hoped this would be soon.

This hope was doomed when she met the new Mrs. Croft at a shop down in Stall Street where Hannah had gone to buy some long gloves for evening wear. The Milsom Street prices did not obtain here, but for the careful shopper the quality was sometimes excellent.

With the aid of Miss Quilling's somewhat rigid taste, she selected six pairs of gloves of spotless white kid and was considering the practicality of an elaborate spider-lace evening shawl worth forty guineas when she heard a musical female voice summon a clerk to the doorway.

Miss Quilling muttered, ''It's young Mrs. Croft, and that dratted female who used to be the prince's mistress.''

"The prince's mistress?" Hannah had been examining her image critically in a hand mirror on the counter. She stopped plucking at the lace of the shawl and raised her eyes to encompass the reflection of the two women who had entered. She was surprised that this news shocked her. Why should she care that Prince Andre had a mistress? It was a habit common enough among lesser men, and heaven knew, princes were particularly susceptible! But red-haired Lady Fiona Westerby had seemed much too mature for His Highness's tastes.

Miss Quilling sniffed. "I couldn't mistake the woman. It was she who commanded you to stand up with the present prince at the Upper Rooms the other night."

"The present prince?"

"Hannah, where are your wits?" She lowered her voice to a biting whisper. "Son of the prince who was her lover."

"Ah." That was better. She found the woman somewhat more attractive. But what was she doing in the company of the Princess Eulalie? Perhaps bearing messages from the princess's former betrothed. Hannah did not doubt that by this time young Mrs. Croft was fully informed of all the details about Hannah's brief stay at Everdene Hall and especially about her quarrel with the prince. Judging by the princess's successful attempt at unseating Hannah during their little race, she would be delighted to learn that Hannah had insulted the prince and run off with one of his horses.

Perhaps this explained her surprising graciousness when she saw Hannah and Miss Quilling. It was she and not Lady Fiona who first recognized Hannah.

"My dear Miss Jasper, how pleasant to see you! Evidently, you are a careful shopper too."

"It is my habit, Your Highness."

Lady Fiona interposed brightly, "What an excellent wife you will make, Miss Jasper! His Royal Highness was saying so only this morning."

Princess Eulalie gave her a quick, sharp glance, but Lady Fiona remained so unconscious of having disturbed her that

Hannah wanted very much to laugh. She restrained the impulse while the princess turned everyone's attention to a more appropriate subject. Her sweet smile bestowed a blessing on "bargains," within limitations.

"Very fair material. One is always aware in such places that they cater for a certain type of bargain seeker, but even you and I could do far worse."

Hannah was coolly amused at this patronizing attitude by a woman so poor that according to common gossip she had been forced to give up the man she loved for the great fortune of a man over three times her age.

"Bargains are no strangers to my family," she boasted to the princess. "My grandfather was a pauper brat. He learned the value of every farthing in a hard school."

"Admirable," Lady Fiona was quick to remind the princess before that lady could utter anything derogatory. "One can see such determination in your brother's splendid, strong face, Miss Jasper. Don't you agree, Your Highness? Such a distinguished man is Captain Desmond!"

"Indeed, yes." Somewhat to Hannah's surprise, the princess revealed a definite interest in Des. Hannah found it understandable that Lady Fiona should praise Des. He was a fine figure of a man, and a hero. But he did not seem to be the princess's type. Nor, indeed, Beau Croft's sort. It was to be expected that the princess would appreciate Beau's looks and, more especially, his subtle mind. However, Her Highness went on enthusiastically.

"The captain is a splendid man. So chivalrous when I . . . so very chivalrous. Does he often attend the balls at the New Assembly Rooms?"

"Upon occasion."

"Does he waltz?"

Hannah hesitated. The waltz was not one of her brother's great accomplishments. He was too big a man to be light on his feet, but he certainly had been taught the skill of this somewhat daring dance, with its handclasp and its bodily contact.

Lady Fiona's laugh trilled through the shop, startling the gentlemanly clerk into dropping the pink satin ribbons he had brought out for Mrs. Croft's perusal.

"Sir Des waltz? I rather think he does. Did I not see him with that pretty Tremoyle child at the Assembly—what you call 'The Upper Rooms'? It was the night Miss Jasper refused a royal command."

The princess blinked. "Oh?"

Lady Fiona went on with her blithe indifference to undercurrents.

"How clever of you, Miss Jasper! You captivated His Highness that night. I do not recall in my memory another young lady who refused to partner him in any set. Yes." She appeared to be thinking it over. "I do believe it was then he determined upon . . ." Smiling mischievously, she broke off. "But I shall say no more on that head. Discretion, you know."

Hannah had her own opinion of the woman's purpose. There was more to it than the apparent desire to annoy Princess Eulalie. Doubtless she was speaking to Hannah, reminding her of the prince's desire to marry her. But nothing in that desire changed the original purpose. He must marry the Jasper fortune. It was most unlikely that the prince, with his spectacular appearance and title, should ever prefer plain Hannah Jasper to his beauteous love, Eulalie Croft. His visit to the Crescent the day after the New Assembly Ball, his intimacy toward her the day Hannah had her accident, and now the fact that she found Lady Fiona in the princess's company all made clear the prince's present close ties to his great love.

"Do you often visit the Assembly Ballrooms, Miss Jasper?" Lady Fiona persisted while Her Highness discussed with the clerk her choice of ribbons for a new bonnet.

"Reasonably so."

Lady Fiona asked suddenly, "But what am I about? We shall see you and Sir Desmond at the Crofts' Waltzing Party, shall we not?"

"I think not." No need to recite the fact that they had received no invitation.

Miss Quilling gave an expressive "Ha!" which attracted Princess Eulalie, who turned to say in pretty perplexity, "But it was my understanding that Sir Desmond, and his sister, of course, would attend our little affair. Have I mistaken Sir Desmond's assurance? My husband, in particular, asked for Miss Jasper. He felt that in a party that seemed so far from his own tastes, poor lamb, he would prefer a few more sedate and settling influences to bear him company. And Miss Jasper, fortunately, is so sensible."

It was Lady Fiona's turn to be displeased. Hannah guessed that for Lady Fiona the chief ornament of the Jasper household was her brother. It would not be surprising. Des made friends easily. One couldn't help liking him.

Hannah agreed that if her brother had given his assurance she would certainly accompany him, though she was amused at the princess's effort to place her in the company of an eighty-five-year-old man.

"How dear of you, Miss Jasper! Mr. Croft and I will be so pleased. My husband's relation, Beaufort, has promised to attend. I know he is by way of being a childhood friend of yours."

She offered her hand. Hannah wondered if she was expected to curtsy but compromised by touching the woman's small, gloved fingers with her own hand. Lady Fiona nodded to Miss Quilling and reminded Hannah, "We trust you will visit us again, Miss Jasper, when we may show you over Everdene. I am persuaded you will be pleased with the improvements."

"Very likely." Hannah added for Mrs. Croft's benefit, "Do give His Highness my respectful good wishes. His presence does honor to Bath."

"I shall indeed convey your wishes, Miss Jasper."

With very little goodwill, Miss Quilling watched them go. She was still muttering her opinion of these fine-feathered creatures when Hannah completed her purchases and they started back up toward the more fashionable area of the town.

The noisy White Hart Inn and Tavern, the hub of activity for the coaching class, loomed up before them and Miss Quilling suggested in her gruff voice, "I had as lief avoid that place. If you've no objection, I daresay we can cross the street here."

Hannah, in a contrary mood, argued that no ill-mannered inmate of a posting house was going to send her running. Several travelers wandered out of the tavern, busy arguing the merits of a recently purchased mare.

The arguing men crossed in front of the two ladies, one man jostling his friend, who was unsteady on his feet. For some reason he carried a partially filled mug of colorless liquid. Under the impact of a shove, the mug spilled over, saturating the front of Hannah's sprigged muslin gown and her silk shawl. Even her morocco slippers were spotted. She cried out and backed away in revulsion and anger. The man who had fallen against her was apparently taking part in a wager concerning the mug. His friend begged the ladies' pardon and would have attempted to scrub off the stains, but Miss Quilling waved him away impatiently. Still mumbling apologies, he followed his unsteady companion.

Hannah had never been more furious. While Miss Quilling clucked and tried in vain to brush her off, the now empty mug went rattling off to a stop between the cobblestones.

A few minutes later, having scrubbed to no purpose, Miss Quilling raised her head, cleared her throat, and when this produced no reaction from Hannah, she motioned frantically.

"Behind you, my girl. A trifle over your left shoulder. His Highness, with that fat General Hoogtrotter."

Hannah rose to her not inconsiderable height, still frantically and vainly scrubbing at her dress.

"Well, I can scarcely prevent that. Let your precious prince see me as I am, in very truth."

Seconds later, looking her most wretched, she found herself surrounded by two gentlemen who had sauntered out of the White Hart, only to find a young lady smelling of the Dutch gin they called "Blue Ruin." She looked flushed and in a distressingly violent mood.

Prince Andre took her nervous hand, stopping its frantic and purposeless stroking. "May I help you, Miss Jasper? Are you feeling quite yourself?"

Hannah's hearing was acute. She did not miss General Hoogstratten's murmured "a trifle disguised. Shouldn't wonder. Gad's life! Strong stuff, that Blue Ruin. Lady, too. Shouldn't have thought it."

The prince ignored him and looked around, still clasping Hannah's hand. He raised his voice.

"You there, with the hackney. Here!"

The hackney coach and horses rattled across the stones from its station before the White Hart Inn and Tavern.

Since it seemed evident that Hannah was much too angry to speak for herself, Miss Quilling explained repressively, "An odious affair. A gentleman wagering how long he could support a mug of . . . that sort . . . in his hand. Fairly foxed, I'll dare swear."

The prince said, "Yes. It is regrettable. Come, Miss Jasper. In you go."

His friend the general was still peering around.

"Don't see the fellow. Are you quite sure, Ma'am? Not but what he exists, but where the deuce has he gone?"

The prince cut him off. "Trotter, I will escort the ladies. Convey my regrets to Her Highness and Lady Fiona. And Trotter . . ."

"Sir?"

"None of your wagging tongue. Do you understand me?"

"Certainly, my boy. That is, Your Highness. Assure you I am not a gossip. Not my sort of thing at all."

Miss Quilling sniffed her opinion of this, and even Hannah, beginning to understand these undercurrents, lost some of her anger in indignation.

"There is nothing to gossip about."

"Of course not, Miss Jasper," the prince assured her, settling her in the musty, unclean interior of the public hackney. "We will have you home and resting in a trice."

"I was not drunk! I do not need rest."

This time the prince's warm, sympathetic smile was unmistakable. "Only a fool would think so. Do not concern yourself. I only meant that after all this hubbub you would want to rest in your own home, in quiet comfort."

Somewhat mollified, she took a long breath, but this only gave her a fresh whiff of her revolting, gin-stained garments. She tried to scramble over to one side of the carriage, but the prince put his hand over hers again, promising, "Do not mind it. I must see to your companion now. Will you be all right?"

"Of course," she snapped, and glared at him as he assisted Miss Quilling into the carriage.

For once, he was dressed like a gentleman, in pale, remarkably well-fitting pantaloons, and a blue coat, which fitted his excellent shoulders as if molded on them. His cravat was exquisitely arranged in one of the complications that were always escaping Desmond. He wore his hat slightly cocked to one side, which gave him a jaunty air, though there remained some indefinable quality that announced his high rank and position.

She would have given much to have prevented his seeing her like this and in front of a tavern, on a public street that was not even in the fashionable heart of Bath. She could only hope his fat friend would scotch any rumors about her "shocking" behavior. The scent was so strong she felt that in itself it made her intoxicated.

With Miss Quilling carefully seated the prince called out "Queen Square!" and went around the carriage. He opened the door and leaped up nimbly to join the ladies from that side, thus placing Hannah between his own body and that of her companion. With revulsion Hannah wondered how either of them could touch her. When her brother, Des, would come home slightly "disguised," as he called it, she would merely look her impatience, sometimes helping his valet get him comfortably to bed. But she had never in all her experience seen a woman of her class in her present condition. It was appalling.

Miss Quilling remained sensible and unruffled. She even carried on a conversation of sorts with Prince Andre across Hannah's shrinking body.

"I trust Your Royal Highness is aware that Miss Jasper visited in Stall Street in order to purchase some gloves. It is quite a respectable street in many ways."

His Highness agreed smilingly.

"I was there in Stall Street myself. We must not refine too much upon this affair. If what you tell me is correct, it was an extremely unusual accident to have occurred where it did. I shouldn't have been nearly so surprised to have seen it happen at the tapster's bar."

"Not to me," Hannah reminded him indignantly. She turned to him on a new note of anger. "And I will thank you, Sir, to refute all such remarks as your own when you hear them."

She had startled him. "I beg your pardon?"

"You very clearly said '*If* what we told you was correct.' Are we to understand that you doubt our word, Quilly's and mine?"

"No, indeed." He actually reddened with embarrassment, she was pleased to note. "I do beg your pardon, Ma'am. And yours, Miss Quilling. I did not mean to imply a doubt."

This was eminently acceptable to the older woman.

"Do be sensible, Hannah. His Highness meant no disrespect."

"None, Miss Jasper. I give you my word. I meant nothing remotely—I would never willingly hurt you. I believe Miss Quilling will assure you of that."

Miss Quilling cleared her throat and agreed hoarsely. "It may be. Yes. Upon reflection, I think you may trust His Highness's word."

"You are very good, Miss Quilling." The prince surprised both women by taking up Quilly's hand and bringing it to his lips.

Hannah was pleased and touched for her friend, but she felt, with some dismay, that this self-centered prince, whose purpose was simply to acquire her fortune, had won over her strongest cohort.

Chapter Eleven

Having dismissed the hackney coach in Queen Square, His Highness strode back to busy Milsom Street, over toward the river and its celebrated Pulteney Bridge. The day was warm, with an occasional breeze, stimulating but gentle, too.

He had always thought of Eulalie in that light but was surprised today by the way Miss Hannah Jasper appeared to him in his mind. True, to date he had found her neither gentle nor sweet, but her peppery character was a constant challenge, and though not beautiful, she was far from unattractive. At the local assemblies and while entertained by hopeful mamas with their rosebud daughters, he had recently been privileged to compare the various candidates for his wife.

He was fully aware of the protocol involved in educating them to what must seem an awesome position. He had every expectation that they would be more conformable than Hannah Jasper, with her pert charm and her air of independence. Their fortunes were comparable to Miss Jasper's, and heaven knew their backgrounds were better. The granddaughter of a Yorkshire pauper thrown upon the parish at the age of five!

Still, she had a natural bearing, a warm, generous mouth in spite of its stubborn quirk, and fine, twinkling hazel eyes that fascinated him even when, as was most of the time, they were angry with him. Perhaps one of her charms was the fact that she did not toad-eat him, which made her different from every person he had ever known except his father and, of course, Eulalie.

But Eulalie was always his unattainable dream. Perhaps even in his happiest moments with her he had sensed that.

He crossed the bridge, stopping to peer out one of the small-paned windows at the river waters flowing below, slightly murky with the browning debris of late summer. The coming of autumn made him think of his own spring-time of happiness, those years in his youth when he and Eulalie had made their plans to return to France, "when that tiresome Directory, with its corruption and inefficiency, shall have been overthrown."

It was Eulalie who insisted that both the recent royal houses of Bourbon, which included the Orleans branch, would prove equally unacceptable to the emancipated citizens of France. It was widely rumored that the senior branch had joined with the Austrian enemy to overthrow the new French Republic, and the junior branch, the Orleans, had disgraced itself by voting the death of its sovereign cousin, Louis XVI.

The theory of Prince Andre's rag-tag followers was that France would be happy to welcome a moderate Valois connection and retain its revolutionary gains.

Alas for such dreams! No one had counted on the rise of a Corsican genius equally adept on the battlefield and in the conference chamber.

"So I must marry money," His Highness reminded himself with all the old repugnance, "or become apprenticed in some profession. But what profession am I suited for? The question produces a lowering answer. None . . . except that I had a great deal of enjoyment out of playing the stable groom."

But most of that pleasure, as he well knew, had come from his choice of a partner in the little game. He could not imagine playing the stable groom with Eulalie or other women in his past life. They would not have been half so delightfully befuddled.

Remembering suddenly that old Trotter had questioned the matter of two invisible men with a gin mug, he increased his speed. It might be necessary to prevent Trotter from spreading hints and rumors. He cursed his own inattention to the matter, but his thoughts had been so completely devoted to the subject of Hannah as his future wife that he hadn't realized the danger until now.

It was still a fair distance to the Sydney Gardens, where he would be meeting Lady Fiona and the princess. The latter had complained that her husband despised all youthful pleasures. She then asked prettily if she might borrow Lady Fiona as escort in those enchanting gardens with their many childish delights, including a labyrinth and music and "adorable cascades."

It seemed harmless, even childlike, and it gave the prince a chance to be in Eulalie's company for an hour or so, properly chaperoned, as though he and his old mentor had come upon the two ladies by chance. At all events, he hoped the meeting would appear a chance affair.

He reached the delightful gardens, which were busy as always, and gave brief, interested attention to the pleasant countryside beyond. It was surprising that at such a moment he should think of the good times he might enjoy riding through that hilly country with Hannah Jasper.

Before he saw Eulalie he heard her musical voice call to him and memory revived. All prosaic thoughts of Hannah Jasper and the other moneyed candidates faded. Through a fountain's spray he made out Eulalie's soft features, the bright tendrils of her hair escaping from her charming straw bonnet, with its blue satin ribbons the color of her eyes. She carried a torn packet of pink satin ribbons in one hand, and he thought how like a little girl those bonnet ribbons would make her look.

"My dear Andre, what delightful chance brought you

here? Lady Fiona, do come and see. General Hoogstratten, it is His Royal Highness.''

The prince came around the fountain, too pleased at sight of her to behave with propriety. He took her hands and kissed the flesh above the wrist. Princess Eulalie, looking roguish, removed her hands from his and clapped them together.

''You have not told us the latest *on-dit*; for you must know, the general has confided that you were on a merciful errand.''

''Shocking affair. Quite shocking!'' the general put in. The prince's eyebrows raised, but the general chattered on. ''Actually, foxed. No other word for it. Forgive me, ladies, but so it was. And so young, too.''

Lady Fiona said, ''I beg pardon, Sir, but Her Highness and I met with Miss Jasper not an hour since, in a mercer's shop, and to my eyes she showed no signs whatever of . . . of what the general saw.''

''Oh, Fiona!'' the princess breathed. ''How can you? You heard the young woman invite herself to our little waltzing party. And there was that unfortunate scene about the wretched grandfather who was what she called 'a pauper brat.' I confess I did not like to credit all that our good General Hoogstratten has been relating to us, but I see now how it was.''

The general's large head bobbed in agreement. ''Poor creature's not used to the attentions from so august a person as His Highness here, and she adopted a little Dutch Courage. Natural enough in someone from that class.''

''A rubbishing story, and I wish you would not repeat it,'' the prince snapped, his happy mood quite ended.

Eulalie's soft, gloved hand stroked the prince's sleeve. ''This defense does you credit, dearest. And nothing more shall be said of the lady's habits. You may trust me not to spread such odious tales.''

''Nor me, I'm sure,'' the general added in a hurry.

The prince could vent his full anger on this tiresome

gabblemonger and did so. "You will do well to keep silent if you and I are to go on together. Now, if it is humanly possible, keep silent for at least five more minutes while Her Highness and I try to enjoy this fine summer day." He offered Eulalie his arm, and she tucked her hand in, closing her fingers warmly about his arm below the elbow. She smiled softly as she gazed up into his face, reading the somber look in his eyes.

"Dearest, someday we shall come about and be together. We have only to wait. How often have I counseled patience?"

"I don't propose to hinge my future on a man's death, if that is what you mean to imply."

The princess's big eyes looked larger with shock.

"But my dear, I meant only in the natural course of life. He is eighty-five, after all is said. Where you came by the horrid idea of an unnatural death I have no notion. I beg you not to hint at such a thing, even for me."

"Unnatural? Who is talking of unnatural—I suppose you mean murder? I meant only—Good God! I beg your pardon, but really, it is the outside of enough."

"What did you mean, then?" she pursued the matter with her wide-eyed concern.

"I don't know, damn it! Yes, I do. I meant that I don't intend to wait around for his death before I make plans for my own future."

"But you must wait. Don't you see, dear? We merely need patience. You must not even dream of . . . of anything else."

He was still frowning but managed to laugh at this advice.

"Not think of marriage? You are far off with that hope, Lalie. I intend to marry as soon as the lady has been properly schooled to what must be expected of her."

"Oh. You were talking of marriage." She dropped his arm and glanced behind her at the general and Lady Fiona, who must have heard every word but were raptly staring at the puffed white clouds overhead.

"Of course I was talking of marriage. How else could I plan for the future? Your husband is not likely to drop dead tomorrow, and I am afraid I cannot afford to wait. Besides, I want to secure my life, to enjoy what others enjoy, a capable wife and a family. Heirs."

She shuddered. When he looked into her face he saw tears there, brimming over. It hurt him to see her blue eyes clouded by pain and in spite of the possible passersby on the leafy path of the Gardens, he kissed the crown of her head quickly, impetuously, feeling almost, if not quite, as he used to feel about her importance in his life.

"Don't cry, dearest. We had the past, the good years when we were young. Now we must look ahead and be practical. You showed me the way by your marriage. That took courage. I only follow your lead."

"Don't say it," she whispered, catching her breath on a sob. "I married a man who must soon leave me free. Your marriage could go on and on forever."

He had to admit to himself that he hoped this was the case. He certainly did not expect his marriage to be a temporary affair.

She seemed to realize there was no more to be said in decency and squinted up at the sun.

"Why did I not take a parasol? That tiresome new maid of mine, she should have seen to it. Samson insists that I take her with me everywhere. One would think I was his prisoner. But of course, when I met Fiona I sent the woman home. There were so many private confidences to be shared"—she gazed up at the prince, blinking away the tears and attempting a smile—"you may imagine about whom."

She was still a child, he thought, a heedless, lovely child who talked of death and murder and flirtations as if she gave them all equal weight. She ran a hand delicately over her throat, ruffling up the high silk collar of her newly fashioned scarf and thrusting the sky-blue scarf aside with an impatient gesture.

"How warm it has grown! Quite oppressive."

It was then that he saw the long, ugly bruise across her collarbone. A black and blue mark, its edges turning a dreadful yellow. Fading.

"How came you by that bruise?" he demanded, hearing the hoarse shock in his voice that made a passing governess with two lively little boys turn to stare at him and then at Princess Eulalie.

The latter covered the bruise with a shaking hand.

"Stupid of me. I did not mean . . . I fell against a . . . an object. So careless. You know how quickly I move, Andre. You yourself were used to say I reminded you of a feather. I have no strength that does not come from you. You know that."

He crushed her fingers between his two palms.

"My poor darling!"

She read something in his face that she obviously did not want to see there. "Promise me you will do nothing. I can manage very well."

"He should be beaten, thrashed!"

"No. In God's name, no! Hush!" She glanced around nervously. "Love me, dearest. Never forget. I can stand anything. Any pain. If only I know I have your love. But I cannot bear it if I think you will do something wild and dangerous to our love."

He found it difficult to speak. "You know I love you."

"Then you will wait, dearest, before you pursue this dreadful marriage to a female who drinks?"

"She does not . . ." He broke off. The argument was pointless. He could not give his one-time beloved the assurance she craved.

What a damned, twisted fiend that old man must be!

At the same time he realized that marriage to Hannah Jasper would not help his poor Eulalie, but he must go on. Perhaps Hannah would join him in his battle against Samson Croft. She did not appear to be a person who would tolerate injustice.

103

Chapter Twelve

It seemed to Hannah vitally important that she should look her best when attending the Crofts' waltzing party even though, as the princess had made plain, Hannah's chief contribution would be to keep Samson Croft's attention occupied. Her new gown, with its appliqued satin trim, had been made in a golden coppery color with a fuller skirt than was fashionable until very recently, and its daring neckline would show her diamond and topaz set to splendid advantage. She knew that the princess would despise topaz stones, but for Hannah they had always been lucky. They complemented her hazel eyes, according to several admirers, and Prince Andre had never seen the topaz set.

Miss Clarissa Tremoyle had assured Hannah excitedly that His Highness would attend. When Hannah asked how she knew this interesting fact, the volatile Clarissa pirouetted down the sitting room, boasting, "I was given a royal command. It was only the country dances, mind, but there I was, being led into the set by a Prince of the Blood. I was all of a tremble, I may tell you."

"What did you speak of?"

Clarissa shrugged. "It is so difficult in the country dances. He asked if I enjoyed Bath, if I had made my come-out, and if I danced the waltz at Almack's. Alas! I had to say I was not yet on such terms with any of the patronesses. You know Mama, she will not be conciliatory. He asked if you were attending the Crofts' party."

"Did he now?" Hannah was more flattered than she wanted to admit, especially to herself. But if she was to show this arrogant young aristocrat that two could play at masquerades, she must find herself in his company more often. It had been a trifle disappointing that he had made no effort to see her after the appalling day in Stall Street. She even wondered if he could have suspected she was drunk—to use the most honest word.

How dared he!

She wished she could make herself irresistible to him. It would teach him how much it hurt to be sought only for her grandfather's fortune. In his case someone must make him understand what it would be like to be sought only for his title and dignities. Hannah Jasper had chosen herself to teach him that salutary lesson.

Hannah arrived at the wide, grassy verge before the Royal Crescent, chaperoned by Beau Croft and, with less enthusiasm, by her brother, Des.

Beau took this occasion to remark, "Have I told you, Hannah, that you are in excellent looks tonight?"

She could not imagine Beau speaking to his new grandmama in such cool terms.

"Thank you. I daresay, we will find Mrs. Croft to be a vision of loveliness."

Any other man would have been discomfited, but Beau let few things overset him. He did smile at her in his saturnine way. "Jealous, Hannah?" When she bristled, he said with flattering certainty, "You needn't be. When I marry one day, it will be no one but you, no matter what you may suspect."

She gave that statement a gusty laugh. "I am not so desperate, dear friend. Nor will I ever be, so you may sleep easily at night."

"All this over a simple compliment?"

"Not at all, Beau. Your princess is exquisite, even when ill treated by her cruel bridegroom."

Des had joined them and looked from one to the other, puzzled. "What is this? Quarreling? I don't like your tone about Her Highness, Hannah. There is nothing amusing in the ill treatment of a fragile creature like Princess Eulalie."

"Mrs. Croft. I should say that would apply to any lady, whether as fragile as Mrs. Croft or otherwise."

"Yes, yes. To be sure. Hannah, I want you to promise you won't behave badly tonight."

"Oh, rubbish!" Men were so incredibly gullible.

They were admitted by a tall, supercilious foreigner in elaborate livery. He seemed to be well acquainted with Beau, and—a matter that troubled Hannah somewhat—acquainted with Des. The liveried footman received the gentlemen unquestioningly, but Hannah, much to her disgust, was treated with deference only as a lady accompanied by two of Mrs. Croft's "usual" guests.

They were ushered up the staircase, past chains of warmly scented roses and greenery, toward Samson and Mrs. Croft at the head of the stairs. On the half-landing, the footman disappeared to repeat his elaborate ceremony with the next guests to arrive. Mrs. Croft looked very like a fairy tale princess in coppery satin over a golden underdress, with yellow diamonds adorning her ears, her hair, and her throat. The necklace was especially heavy, concealing a considerable portion of her slender neck.

All this was of little importance to Hannah, who noticed at once that the princess's costume was very near in color to the gown Hannah had chosen with great difficulty for herself. Although the princess must have noticed this too when Hannah's furred satin pelisse was removed before she had mounted the stairs, she gave no indication, perhaps because her attention was devoted to the gentlemen accompanying Hannah.

Old Samson leaned heavily upon a walking stick, but one hand was extended to his guests, a strong, callused hand.

Hannah could not help wondering if that hand was guilty of cruelty to his lovely wife after all. Samson wasted no time or attention upon his grandson, and treated Des with embarrassing contempt, saving his real enthusiasm for Hannah.

He bowed stiffly over her hand, and his fierce gaze brightened as he examined her slender form. She had always carried herself well, and some of her natural grace was attributable to her quaint independent air, so much at variance with the delicate fashions of the polite world.

"Well, luv, ye've done yourself proud. If that look don't win your precious prince, naught will do the job."

Despite her gratitude, she colored, wishing his harsh voice had not carried with such piercing effect. His wife stopped fanning herself but did not look their way. She had been using her silk fan to good effect while she charmed Desmond. Somewhat to Hannah's surprise, Beau hadn't lingered and was in the doorway of the ballroom, dazzling Clarissa Tremoyle with his flattery.

A dozen guests were strolling about the long drawing room, which adjoined the ballroom, while several of Samson's old friends had settled themselves in the little card room beyond. They looked to be preparing for a faro bank, since faro ranked considerably higher in Samson's eyes than dancing.

Hannah thanked her flattering host, who held her hand in a hard grasp while he asked, "What's this? Blushes from a sensible lass like yourself? Tell me, are ye truly hanging out for a title? Would it make 'e happy then?"

His wife's fan remained perfectly still. Hannah could hear her brother's sonorous deep voice replying to some remark of hers about 'fallen glories she had known as a child.' Des was all sympathy, forgetting that the princess had been two years old when her French mother fled with her across the channel to safety and poverty at a lodging house in Folkestone. Before this time, for the first two years of her life, Princess Eulalie had been reared in the uncertain financial care of her mother's French relations, who favored the bourgeois activities of the New French National Assembly. Her Bavarian relations had never even seen her until she was established with the pretentious little "Valois Court" in England.

Hannah caught Samson Croft's eye. He lowered his voice to remark wisely, "We all be prisoners to our dreams, eh, me girl?"

"Very true, Sir."

"And ye're silly as the rest. Ye've a notion to be a princess."

She would have denied this vigorously, but the presence of the eavesdropping Mrs. Croft drove her to further Samson's mistaken idea of her. "Why not, Sir? People marry for many reasons. Some for a pretty face. Some for a great fortune. Some even for a title."

He appreciated the barbs in that and smiled grimly. It was interesting to note that even at his age he seemed to possess all his teeth, which he exhibited with his smile.

"Ye're on the mark there. Well, so be it. If ye've a notion to buy a prince, don't ye be letting others talk ye from it. I never did. And I bought me four wives to prove it."

In the general way of things, such an admission must be ignored. However, Samson Croft did not fall into any category but his own, and Hannah yielded to her natural impulse. She laughed.

"Of course, Sir. But forgive me if I trust I shall not need to go so far. Four husbands? No, I thank you."

"What, Miss Jasper?" Eulalie Croft asked brightly. "Four husbands? You are indeed ambitious."

Hannah was wise enough not to pursue this malice. She pretended to regard the remark as lively and absurd, unworthy of notice. She laughed, tapped Desmond's arm with her own brise fan, warning him.

"Take care. Mrs. Croft is in fine form tonight."

She went on toward the twittering, chattering little groups in the ballroom with her smile carefully frozen upon her face. The small orchestra of three, preparing for the dancing, emitted squeaks, squawks, and cat cries in one far corner, partially concealed by potted ferns.

Beau Croft and young Miss Tremoyle, now chaperoned by Clarissa's complaisant mama, continued their animated conversation, and Hannah, not for the first time, was struck by the knowledge of Beau's opportunism. She wondered if she could be jealous, but it hardly seemed possible. His close presence in the carriage had meant no more to her than that of Des on her other side. He was a friend, a comrade. Untrustworthy, often a liar, but on many occasions he had defended her, taken the blame, pretended to be Hannah, and only her insistence on owning up to childhood mischief had saved him from her punishment.

But she would never love him. Being with him was comfortable. Not exciting or challenging or maddening.

She replied absently to one of her admirers, a friend of Desmond's. Quiet, gentle Sir Nigel Sedgecombe had dangled after her for the past two years, both in Bath and in London, but she had long ago learned that the Sedgecombe estates were heavily encumbered. He needed to marry money.

She stared across the room at the long windows, the rich blue of their velvet portières so flattering to the young females present, and to Eulalie Croft. The colors brought back memories of the day Hannah had ridden Rob-Roy up past these apartments and playfully fenced with the "groom" before the disastrous disclosure of his real identity. There had been that other day, when she was walking and he appeared so suddenly, charming her with his impudence. How happy life would have been if Prince Andre-Charles et cetera had remained "Michael Meiggs"!

And suddenly, amid a flurry of excitement, the swish of taffeta and silk gowns, the buzz of voices, her delightful "stablegroom" appeared just behind Sir Nigel. A moment's reflection reminded her that she resented His Highness fiercely.

In view of her resentment, she thought he must have deliberately made himself appear to his best advantage. His flawless evening attire, the perfectly fitted coat, and the snowy white folds of his neckcloth only accentuated the excitement of his eyes and sensuous mouth, the sculptured bone structure of his face that she had never really noticed before.

As part of her revenge, she had intended to show an interest in him. This proved embarrassingly easy. She was amused to note two facts: first, that his hostess, Eulalie Croft, had left her post out in the gallery above the staircase and taken his arm, and second, that Prince Andre's attention was definitely centered upon Hannah herself. His gaze never left her face.

Hannah flashed a happy smile, careful to exclude all signs of the petulance she had demonstrated at their last meeting. By an accident of timing, perhaps maneuvered by her husband, Mrs. Croft was called back to greet another guest at just the moment that the prince bowed to Hannah.

"Miss Jasper." He looked her over from head to foot, and even her suspicious nature allowed that what he saw he admired. "You leave me breathless."

She curtsied, demure and modest. "Your Royal Highness is too kind."

"Not kind enough, m'dear," Sir Nigel put in, trying to retrieve the close position he had lost upon the prince's arrival.

The prince found a use for this as well. "He is quite right, you know, Miss Jasper. You are looking far too beautiful for mere words."

Hannah frowned. He must think her an absolute fool. Did all women of his acquaintance believe such absurdities?

"That will do. I don't hold with nonsensical exaggerations."

For some obscure reason, this made the prince laugh. Sir Nigel followed with his own small titter, though Hannah was certain he did not know why the prince laughed. His Highness raised both hands in surrender.

"Well, then, my tastes are unorthodox. Very much those of a good stablegroom, in fact."

Hannah raised her eyes to heaven but couldn't restrain a smile.

Sir Nigel, however, was shocked. "Really, Sir! Not a stablegroom!"

The prince turned to him. "I do believe that lovely creature is attempting to attract you, my lucky friend. Do not disappoint her."

The lovely creature, as Hannah saw at once, was Lady Fiona Westerby, looking resplendent in green with an impressive grass-green feathered arrangement waving above her red hair. Sir Nigel raised his quizzing glass, surveyed the lady. Satisfied that the personage was worth his attention, he bowed to Hannah, excused himself, and strolled across the room. Though Lady Fiona's moist-lipped invitation had been clear enough, her eyes lingered over the sight of Captain Sir Desmond Jasper, who was now pausing in the spacious doorway to survey the scene without much interest. No old cronies here in the ballroom. He glanced longingly toward the card room.

Meanwhile, a lackey, looking uncomfortable in the livery of Princess Eulalie's Bavarian ancestral house and carrying a tray of champagne, appeared at the prince's side. The latter took two glasses, offered Hannah one of them, and murmured with his mischievous "stablegroom" look, "I am persuaded that your friend Meiggs would drink to our closer acquaintance."

"Possibly. He was an impudent fellow." She raised the glass, her eyes laughing. Perhaps they borrowed some of the sparkle of the wine. For an instant his gaze traveled from the glass to her lips. Then he saluted her with his own glass. But during that instant she had a dreadful, self-conscious fear that he remembered the episode with the Blue Ruin.

She sipped the champagne, then reminded him in a voice pitched slightly higher than her usual tone, "I assure you,

Sir, I am not about to empty the glass at once. It is not Blue Ruin, after all."

She saw that she had startled him. She felt that his laugh was forced.

"Indeed, Miss Jasper, your friend the stablegroom was actually thinking something only indirectly related to wine. Or Blue Ruin if it comes to that. He was wondering what it would be like to kiss the champagne off your lips."

It was a relief to hear the orchestra strike up a tune, anything to take the attention from herself. She wished she had a free hand to cover her cheeks. She knew she must have turned red as fire.

A vagrant thought did run through her head—I really must wear this color more frequently.

It might, of course, be the way the crisp golden brown curls of hair had been arranged in the Grecian style around her piquant face, with bronze silk ribbons laced through the coiffure. But he was still looking at her mouth, a fact that made her excessively uncomfortable.

She bit her lip, finding it hard not to laugh out of nervous embarrassment.

"Dear me, one can only be relieved that the stable-groom is far away at this moment. His Highness has far superior manners; isn't it so?"

"His Highness sounds a dull dog to me." He glanced down the room at the potted ferns. "When do they play a waltz?"

"Presently." She saw that Lady Fiona had basely deserted Sir Nigel and was moving toward Desmond. That made her more uneasy. She was not at all sure the mistress of a dead prince could have a genuine interest in her brother.

Desmond was very dear to her, but like her, he was neither strikingly handsome, nor irresistably charming. The advantage he did have was an annual income of above fifteen thousand pounds. And unlike Hannah, he had always "sported the brunt" freely, without counting the cost.

"She will not eat him, you know," Prince Andre reminded her. She fancied she heard a tinge of resentment in his voice, not surprisingly. The woman was his friend and confidante. There was another factor involved. Both His Highness and Lady Fiona probably shared a common interest, the Jasper fortune.

"He is very naive," she explained, and sipped her champagne.

The prince frowned. "I don't think I quite understand. Fiona is simple enough in her desires. The mature male of more physical than mental attainments. That is all she asks of life."

His frankness surprised her. It was not gallant of him, but it might well be true.

"An apt description of Desmond," she confessed.

She became aware that unlike in the balls she was used to, dancing had opened with the waltz. The blue ballroom suddenly came alive with movement. Several pairs of dancers around her whirled away, and the prince, without taking his eyes from her face, put one arm around her waist.

"Come."

She was conscious of an excitement out of all proportion to his simple touch. It was maddening and quite ruined all her dreams of her own masquerade. She must not, on any account, fall in love with this roguish prince. Resistance to his touch, however, was more difficult.

Before she could draw away or permit him to sweep her into the dance she became aware of a large obstacle, General Hoogstratten, puffing a little as he led Eulalie Croft to Prince Andre.

"Honored to act in such a capacity. Sir, since Your Highness, as the person of first consequence present, will open the dancing with your hostess, I have the pleasure of Miss Jasper's company."

Hannah looked at Eulalie Croft, whose big-eyed innocence infuriated her. At the same time she heard the prince's sotto voce muttering, "Hoog, you've run your length with this business."

For Hannah good manners won the battle. There was nothing for it but to accept the fat general's hand, close her gloved fingers in his, and be thumped away into the dance.

She gazed back over her partner's shoulder and saw with infinite pleasure that the prince looked pale, angry, and appeared to be deep in a low-voiced argument with his princess.

Meanwhile, the general babbled on, obligingly answering his own questions as to whether Hannah enjoyed the evening, and why she and her brother chose to spend more than half their year in Bath when there were so many pleasures awaiting them in London and Brighton among the Regent's Carlton House Set.

He tugged her around the room, heavily attempting to keep time to the music, but she had the distinct impression that his interest in her was no greater than hers in him. Luckily, only half the dance remained, and that was soon ended. They found themselves near one of the trays of champagne cups. The general obligingly signaled to the lackey and offered nothing to Hannah. For himself he took up a glass of champagne.

"Thank you, sir," she told him, wondering if his gesture was deliberate. Did he think she would behave badly, become "bosky" or "foxed," as her brother would say? It seemed to her that everything tonight aroused her sensitivity. "Champagne, if you please."

The general capped his first awkwardness by hesitating. "Of course. Only thought—my mistake, Ma'am." He gave her his champagne. Was he determined to watch every sip she took?

She was relieved when Beau Croft came to her with the totally false reminder, "Our waltz, Hannah."

She welcomed the rescue. "So it is. Forgive me, General."

Hannah turned away, setting down her glass. When she looked at Beau Croft again he had been inexplicably transformed to Prince Andre-Charles, smiling as innocently as the beauteous Mrs. Croft could have smiled.

"Our dance, I believe?"

She made no struggle to avoid temptation, reminding herself that she must play the eager, prospective "princess" if she was to give her ultimate refusal its proper weight. But that time might be long in coming, since she was sure to enjoy her masquerade much too well.

His Royal Highness imagined that any female would be delighted to trade her fortune for his title. He should be taught that one female, at least, required more of a man.

"How well suited we are!" she murmured, looking up with romance in her eyes.

His own eyelids flickered as though he hadn't expected quite so much honey so soon after a few of her usual sharp setdowns. He even looked a trifle suspicious, but he dipped and swung her around with as much abandon as her narrow skirts would permit, and gave every sign of enjoying the feel of her in his arms. His fingers tightened a trifle around her waist, but she was far from objecting to that. Truth to tell, she could hardly remember a dance she had enjoyed more. In a country dance or a cotillion, and certainly in a minuet, she and her partner were too absorbed in a kind of athletic competition with the others in their set, and Hannah's experience with the waltz had been chiefly confined to partners who were old friends or dangling after an heiress or simply shy.

His Royal Highness was neither an old friend nor shy. Hannah had anticipated the experience with him, and she was right. A waltz in his arms made her head whirl fully as much as the rest of her slim figure while they dipped, circled the floor, and moved with a grace that even Hannah could not deny, for all her level-headed view of her own charms.

It was a glorious business and over much too soon. When the music ended with a flourish, Prince Andre's cheek happened to be close to the curls piled Greek-fashion above her ear, and she could not mistake the fact that his lips touched her hair.

A moment later, still holding her close, he murmured, "We deal remarkably well together. Have you taken note of that?"

"Stuff!" she whispered, trying to give the word a stern edge. She found herself in hearty agreement with him but wouldn't dream of saying so until she remembered that he would expect her to be persuadable, if she was going to be his prospective bride.

She compromised by smiling sweetly into his face as he brought her to the Lady Fiona and General Hoogstratten, who stood gossiping while they sampled pâtés and several of the small cakes for which Bath had a certain fame.

With a rueful laugh Lady Fiona complained, "Miss Jasper, is there no way to draw that sturdy brother of yours back to the ballroom? Or at all events, to the dining room?"

"Shouldn't think he'd object, Ma'am," the general put in. "Looks to me a good trencherman, and there is a deal to choose from in the dining room. The princess always did know what would tempt a man's appetite."

Hannah looked out at the gallery. "Not Des, I'm afraid. He dotes on piquet. Or, if there are more players involved, he is a great faro devotee."

The lady looked as though she might sweep into the card room herself in search of Des.

At the same time His Highness remarked to Hannah, "I had no notion Captain Jasper's powers of attraction were so great. He must confide to me his secret someday." Before she could reply he added, "I had better lure him away from the cards or I'm very much afraid the last shreds of Fiona's reputation will be forever lost."

She was amused but also sorry to see him go. Whether stablegroom or prince, his presence exercised a thrilling effect upon her.

This did not prevent her from urging him cheerfully, "Please, do so. If we must all suffer so much violent prancing and flitting about, then my brother must also do his part.''

The prince laughed, agreed, and went out to drag in the reluctant Sir Des.

Beau Croft, on his way to the dining room with a giggling, happy Clarissa Tremoyle, stopped close to Hannah. While Clarissa remained radiant under the General's good-natured attentions, Beau warned Hannah, his sardonic voice low but audible to her, ''Take care, my girl. I watched you in the dance. Our princeling will soon have a fortune in his pretty paws.''

The remark infuriated Hannah, partly because, with unerring skill, Beau had struck at her most vulnerable spot. She found herself resenting Beau's interference also because it was so insulting to His Highness. This realization shocked her.

It had seemed to her during the waltz that her partner's behavior indicated an attraction to her that transcended the mere dangling after a rich wife. He had not been in nearly such good spirits earlier in the evening when he had been accosted by the princess, who was said to be his great, unrequited love. She refused to be persuaded of the prince's perfidy, even by the cynical Beau.

His Highness appeared in the doorway with Desmond. He had a firm grip on the latter's arm, very much like a warder with a prisoner, and was laughing at his companion's dry comment.

At the same time Eulalie Croft and her husband approached the doorway from the dining room. She had her hand on her husband's arm and seemed startled to encounter Des and the prince so abruptly. She drew back, pulling her hand away from Samson.

The nervous and unexpected motion caused her to clutch at her throat. The threads stringing her exquisite necklace of yellow diamonds snapped in her fingers. The broken string fell to the gallery floor with a hard, chunky sound, but during the first moments, none of the guests in the immediate vicinity noticed the dazzling stones.

Des, the prince, and Hannah stared.

The loss of the necklace disclosed what appeared to be a wide, highly colored bruise, like the mark of a lash across her throat. It crossed an older bruise already turning a yellow-ocre in color.

It was Des who spoke up in breathless horror. "By Gad, Ma'am, you're hurt!"

The princess covered the bruises with a hand that shook perceptibly.

"Dreadful, I know. I was out riding. A horrid branch loomed up quite out of nowhere and snapped across—Oh! It should never have been seen." With a ghastly cheerfulness she raised her voice. "Will some gentleman bring me a glass of champagne? I feel the need of . . . of . . ."

Prince Andre reached past Hannah and signaled to a lackey with a tray.

Hannah was the only one who looked at Samson Croft. His rugged face showed no signs of remorse or anger but only a thoughtful interest in the scars. Curiosity, Hannah decided. But whether he was puzzled over the source of the bruises or over his wife's reaction, it was hard to say.

Des remained speechless, red with indignation. Hannah sensed that in another instant he would say something unthinkable and shocking. She crossed between Des and Prince Andre, shaking her brother's arm. "Des, not one of your migraines again? Oh, dear." Over her shoulder she told Samson and Eulalie, "My poor brother. I am afraid we must leave. Desmond has these occasional attacks. They began in the West Indies, you know, when he was injured defending his ship against two French frigates."

Des recovered his good manners with an effort. "Good Lord, Hannah! Nothing of the sort."

All the same, he allowed Hannah to nudge him along the gallery to the staircase. He was still looking back. The princess's fingers played nervously over her bruises, the very gesture of concealment calling new attention to them. When Hannah too looked back, she surprised a grim smile on Samson Croft's harsh mouth. He nodded to her. She couldn't even guess what that meant.

After a startled minute or two Prince Andre strode after the Jaspers. Des was leaning over the balustrade to summon a butler on the floor below. Having located the man, he bellowed for his sister's wraps.

Meanwhile, the prince had taken Hannah's fingers and brought them to his lips. He confided quietly, "I understand your brother's feelings. I share them. But Her Highness assures me the bruises are self-inflicted, the result of accidents. We can do nothing until she admits the truth."

"The truth?" she repeated coolly. "Why should you doubt Mrs. Croft's assurance? I do not."

She drew her hand out of his grasp and walked down the stairs with Des, leaving a puzzled, frowning prince behind, staring after her.

Chapter Thirteen

Since they had gone on so well at the Waltzing Party, Hannah expected to have the prince or his followers engage her time for the purpose of furthering his pursuit. Perversely enough, she heard nothing from them until Lady Fiona Westerby came calling one day to ask her advice upon the best drapers and carpeting warehouse in the area.

"So bothersome for one who is not to be the mistress of the house, my dear Miss Jasper. His Highness's bride should, of course, select those items. But so it is. I am to choose."

"Then His Highness is planning marriage?" Hannah inquired more calmly than she felt. She told herself her disappointment was due to the collapse of her plan for revenge. She could not now bring him to the point of marriage and then cry off, as she had intended, if he had chosen another rich bride.

Lady Fiona kept looking toward the double doors of the little back parlor, with its crimson velvet hangings that were too heavy for a morning in late summer. It was a cozy room, in general, but Lady Fiona's presence made it smaller, stifling. The lady moved too much, swayed and stretched in an effort to see someone or some thing enter, and Hannah had little doubt that the object of Lady Fiona's attention was Desmond Jasper.

At Hannah's repeated question, Lady Fiona laughed

lightly. "His Highness certainly plans marriage, but it must depend upon the lady. . . . What was I saying? Ah. The carpets at Everdene. You are needed, Miss Jasper. His Highness would not wish a choice made without your approval."

"Mine! I cannot conceive how it is an affair of mine." But her heart leaped delightedly. He still expected to make her his wife. Since this idea was so pleasing, she hastily reminded herself that his arrogant self-assurance made her masquerade much easier.

"I wonder, Miss Jasper, if you and your heroic brother would be kind enough to visit Everdene soon. A morning visit if you prefer, but I am persuaded you would need more time. His Highness will require so much advice."

"Perhaps."

An engagement having been made, Lady Fiona was about to depart when she saw Desmond's powerful figure approach across Queen Square. Watching her, Hannah wondered if the woman was actually attracted to Des. She had certainly changed color, perhaps only a trifle, but indicative of genuine feelings. Lady Fiona moistened her lips and drew herself up to look her best in the narrow silhouette of the year's fashions.

Hannah concealed her sympathetic smile. When Mrs. Plackett, the housekeeper, opened the door to Des, Lady Fiona had backed away to the staircase beside Hannah. The latter supposed that the lady wished to spend just a few more minutes with Des than were possible if she encountered him in the doorway.

He came in explosively, not even noticing Lady Fiona for a few seconds.

"Hannah, you will not credit it. I want to talk to you. An outrage. By Gad, an outrage!"

Hannah remained calm under this onslaught.

"Yes, dear, later. Lady Fiona has been kind enough to call upon us with an invitation."

"To be sure. Servant, Your Ladyship . . . Hannah, have

you been to the Abbey anytime these past three nights? The Abbey Yard, I should say.''

She and Her Ladyship exchanged glances. At the same time Hannah thought Lady Fiona did not look quite so surprised. Was this something she knew already? Hannah said, ''I haven't been at the Abbey since Sunday. On our way to the Pump Room this morning and yesterday as well, Quilly and I crossed very near to the Abbey Yard. How does this concern you, Des? You refused to accompany us.''

''No, no. In the early night, I say. About the time you would be taking tea of an evening.''

''Then I am certainly taking tea. Lady Fiona, my brother is not usually so rag-mannered, but he seems to be in a towering rage over some absurd . . . what, Des?''

''No such thing. But I heard a rumor at the White Hart. Some preposterous tale started by God knows who—beg pardon, Your Ladyship.''

''I understand perfectly, Sir,'' that lady assured him, moving forward. ''But such rumors are best scotched by laughter, an amused dismissal.'' She offered him her hand, which he took in an abstracted way while complaining.

''And so I would have done, in the ordinary way. But a man's own sister, it is too much! I'd have given the fellow a leveler, but he was such a milksop I was afraid I would break his jaw. He was very near to cowering behind the tapster's bar, I can tell you.''

Lady Fiona smiled up sympathetically into his strained features.

''I'll wager he will never utter such rubbish again.'' She looked over at Hannah. ''You are fortunate in having so gallant a champion, Miss Jasper.''

''I know that.''

''Then I will take my leave. Good day to you both.''

She reached the door, which the housekeeper opened for her with almost insulting haste. Mrs. Plackett signaled the prince's stablegroom, Meiggs, who brought the prince's carriage and team up to meet Lady Fiona. Apparently, the man had many talents and looked quite capable of coaching the vehicle. Or was Prince Andre in such a bad way that it was necessary for his servants to double their duties? Mrs. Plackett was just closing the door with sniffs of disapproval at the lady's obvious interest in Sir Desmond when they all heard Lady Fiona's wild shriek.

Des rushed out to the shallow steps with Hannah hard on his heels. They found Meiggs straining to control the team of neat bays upset by Lady Fiona's shriek. The lady herself had turned her ankle on a stone and fallen into the arms of Desmond's groom, Jemie.

She raised her head with difficulty, giving Des a valiant, pain-wracked smile.

"Do not concern yourself, Sir." She caught her breath, murmured, "It is nothing," then winced, and went on with great effort, "A mere . . . sprain."

Des elbowed Jemie out of the way and took his place, kneeling beside her in the street while Hannah watched with interest and considerable curiosity. Des looked over the lady's feathered green bonnet commanding Mrs. Plackett. "Bring me Hannah's *sal volatile*, whatever you can find."

"I don't have smelling salts, dear." Hannah hadn't fainted since she was five and fell off the barn roof. She saw Lady Fiona's eyelids flutter. She did not miss the indignant glance that lady shot at her, but quickly hid her own amusement in an elaborate pretense of sympathy.

"Des, carry the lady indoors. She should be kept warm. There may be broken bones, and shock. Heavens! Move!"

This time there was a definite smile on Lady Fiona's not unattractive face, but being intelligent as well, she diluted the smile with a groan.

"Too kind . . . Perhaps . . . a brief period of rest."

"Certainly," Hannah agreed. "Mrs. Plackett, the green chamber, I think. It is very bright and cheerful this time of year. And is there any *sal volatile* in the house?"

Mrs. Plackett restrained her annoyance. Like Hannah, she understood exactly what their guest was about.

"My own, certainly, Miss Hannah. This way, Master Desmond."

Lady Fiona had finally succeeded in making an impression upon Desmond Jasper. He surprised even Hannah by fussing about the "sick room" during the next hour, repeatedly putting his head in at the doorway to inquire "if Your Ladyship is feeling more the thing."

After several of these loud and rather obvious tiptoed visits, he stepped into the room, walking as lightly as his powerful physique would allow, and began to make conversation that Hannah thought quite inane, but Lady Fiona received it all with sparkling charm and a flattering interest. She seemed vastly entertained by Desmond's description of a fight between two sailors off Jamaica, during which the bo'sun's mate slipped on the rain-wet deck and sprained his ankle "the very same as yours, Ma'am . . . well, not precisely the same, but you understand what I mean to say."

"Indeed I do, Sir," the lady assured him, and laughed heartily, as was seemly to a man of Desmond's notions that females were fragile, delicate, and the soul of propriety at all times.

When Hannah came in to find Desmond half seated at the end of the green-and-gold-cushioned chaise longue, he arose quickly, with an embarrassed laugh.

"Afraid that wasn't quite the thing, Ma'am, but your conversation—I might say—intoxicating."

"My very thought, Sir, when I listened to your fascinating account of your experiences at sea. Ah, Miss Jasper. You may see in what case I find myself. And we have your brother to thank for it. He is all that is amiable."

"Nothing, really," he disclaimed. "Hannah, don't you think Lady Westerby would be the better for a small glass of whatever the devil you ladies drink at this hour?"

Hannah looked a question, which Lady Fiona answered at once. "I wonder if there is just a drop of that Spanish sherry available. Much too strengthy, as they say, but it had an excellent effect upon me once, after I was beset by the importunities of an exiled count, an acquaintance of His Late Highness—'' She broke off in pretty confusion. ''But His Highness had no notion of the count's true nature.''

Desmond agreed at once and went to the Jasper cellars personally to supervise the search for an exceptional bottle of the sherry, which had not, heretofore, been among his own favorites.

Meanwhile, having caught Her Ladyship alone for this brief time, Hannah decided she had finally gotten her chance to discuss a matter that seemed to concern herself.

''Your Ladyship, what was my brother's quarrel about?''

''Quarrel? Quarrel? I've no notion.'' Lady Fiona fidgeted, carefully lifting her bandaged foot to another position. Her fine eyes avoided Hannah, who had no intention of being fobbed off so easily.

''Des nearly gave some milksop a facer. Or was it a leveler, as Des describes it? Why?''

Her Ladyship licked her lips. ''I have no way of knowing.'' Her uneasy gaze leaped from Hannah to the doorway, but there was still no sign of Desmond. She breathed deeply, seeing no escape from Hannah's stern pressure. ''I believe there was a rumor that you had been seen before Bath Abbey, a trifle—disguised.''

''Drunk.''

''Horrid word. No. It was all a hum. A nothing. A jest of some humorous fellow meaning merely to create a diversion.''

''And how does it come about that you have heard this lie; for lie it is, Ma'am?''

Lady Fiona was clearly flustered.

''I—I cannot be certain, Miss Jasper. It was talked of yesterday and this morning, because of the original event outside the White Hart. Naturally, I gave it the lie.''

''Naturally. And I may assume that since you yourself did not spread this new story, it was spread by General Hoogstratten." She paused several seconds. "Or by His Royal Highness."

"No. Never. The general is presently in London with commissions to complete for His Highness. And as for His Highness spreading such a tale—impossible."

"But he did not deny either story when he heard it."

"Well . . ." Lady Fiona looked uncomfortable. "One never knows how these things are spread, but I am persuaded you must be misinformed. His Highness—I recall distinctly—he defended you on the very morning the original episode occurred."

"Defended me to whom?" As Her Ladyship continued to look puzzled, Hannah explained with glittering sharpness. "To earn a defense one must be attacked. I make no doubt General Hoogstratten was one of my attackers, since he saw the incident and claimed he did not see the man who spilled the gin upon me."

"You are speaking of that day nearly a fortnight ago. The matter was mentioned."

"We are very carefully avoiding the lady I believe to be back of this business. Including the preposterous story about me on the Abbey steps."

Lady Fiona began a stammered protest, through which Hannah caught the note of panic. "She and Mr. Samson Croft have been in Yorkshire since the night of the Waltzing Party. But even if she were in Bath, what reason has she for such an act? She has a settled life now, totally removed from His Highness. It would be to no purpose."

Not if she is still in love with Prince Andre, Hannah thought, and went on to ask the details of the latest lie being spread about herself. Here she received no help. Lady Fiona did not have any details. Even Desmond was vague when he came in at that moment, followed by the Jaspers' only footman, carrying a tray, glasses, and a decanter.

"Least said, soonest mended," Desmond remarked, and indicated the decanter. "Shall it be Spanish sherry for you, Hannah?"

"No, thank you. Des, what are they saying about me?"

"I'm damned—beg pardon, Your Ladyship—deuced if I know. It was just a muddled remark, but it set me all afire, I may tell you." He poured for Lady Fiona while he insisted, "It is perfectly clear to me. That tuppenny prince saw you and gossiped to every chattermonger in Bath."

"I vow, Sir Desmond, it is nothing of that sort." Lady Fiona sprinkled a drop of the pale golden wine and then, waving the Waterford glass, reminded Hannah, "You see? Here, I have spilled wine. Doubtless, an enemy would say I am . . . what is the term, Sir? I am bosky."

"All nonsense, Ma'am. Not on a sip of sherry."

Hannah was even more decisive. Since those she suspected were not in Bath and could not have spread this latest rumor, very likely it had been an accident, a coincidence, even someone who resembled her. "I suggest we turn the subject. I am sick to death of this tiresome business. I have never been drunk, bosky, disguised, or any other cant expression. But I make no doubt there are those who would like to see me one of those things."

She was perceptive enough to realize that both Des and Lady Fiona had many more interesting, if less monumental, matters to talk of than the lies spread about herself. She made an excuse and left them to discuss Desmond's seafaring career.

Early in the afternoon, before the Jaspers' dinner, which was served earlier than in sophisticated London, Mrs. Plackett came up to inform Hannah.

"Her ladyship's carriage has come. An open barouche, Miss Hannah. The coachman is waiting belowstairs."

Hannah arose, tossing aside some highly uninteresting petitpoint that she had been working between yawns.

"Tell him he must wait in the servants' quarters or out in the square. The weather seems adequate."

"That's as may be," Mrs. Plackett agreed, rolling her eyes. "But I fear me, the—ah—person prefers to wait inside, at the foot of the staircase. Insists, if the truth be known.''

Hannah sighed. ''Then *I fear me* we must come to fisticuffs if all else fails.''

''Miss Hannah!''

''You know quite what I mean.'' Hannah passed Mrs. Plackett with a firm step and a determination to show at least one person today that she was still mistress of this house and in no way a creature who took Dutch gin when all else in her life failed.

At the head of the staircase she stopped abruptly.

There he was, exactly as he had stood more than a fortnight ago, a trim, unbelievably attractive stablegroom—or was he now a coachman?—in wide, torn sleeves, a leather jerkin, patched breeches, and dusty boots.

It was too absurd. She had to laugh. But with considerable zest she entered into his little game.

''So your master sent you to take up Lady Westerby.''

''Yez'll have the right of it there, Ma'am. He sent me, seeing as how you was always more like to bid me welcome than His Highness.''

''Highly probable. You appear to be of more use in the world than your ramshackle prince.''

Although the light in his eyes told her he enjoyed this verbal tussle, he questioned with a great show of dignity, ''Ramshackle? Well, then, Ma'am, 'pon honor, His Highness is a sweet goer and easy to the harness.''

She leaned over the balustrade. ''But not, I fear, of any use in the lengthy run. It's my opinion he could not clear the first hurdle.''

He grinned. ''Try him on the straight course, Ma'am.'' He was so ingratiating she wondered whether she could resist him. But this she must do. She kept firmly in mind that her fortune and not she was the object of all this charm.

She backed away from the balustrade.

''Very well, then. I will inform Lady Westerby that His Highness's barouche is awaiting her.''

For the first time she seemed to ruffle him. He moved to the newel post, looking up at her coaxingly.

"Ah, but 'tis yourself His Highness sent me for. If I was to take up the Lady Fiona and not yourself, there be no knowing how I'd fare with my prince, him that yourself calls ramshackle. There might even be beatings."

"I'm sure His Highness will show you all the consideration you deserve," she warned him, and was about to refuse his coaxing when Des came out to the stairhead to see what all the chatter was about.

"Now, see here," he warned the prince, "you be off. I'll give escort to Lady Westerby myself. Tell your master—good Lord!"

"Michael Meiggs," Hannah presented the prince to her brother. "You do remember, Des. He came several weeks ago with an invitation from his master, Prince Andre-Charles."

"Yes, but—good Lord!" Des looked at his sister in perplexity, saw that she was in one of her odd humors, and gave up the struggle to explain the prince's curious double identity. "I collect, this is something exquisitely humorous that you two are about. I don't pretend to understand it." He turned away, then gave one parting shot. "But I shall escort Lady Westerby."

"If you must, you must," the prince agreed, all too promptly. "And Miss Jasper?" he persisted.

Des raised his voice. "My sister has told you she is not interested in a visit. I absolutely forbid it. You may convey that to your—er—to yourself."

It needed only this! Hannah leaned over the stairrail.

"Very well. A short visit. No more than fifteen—half an hour. You will wait in the kitchen. Mrs. Plackett, please show Michael Meiggs to the kitchen."

The impudent fellow saluted her flippantly.

"You are all kindness, Ma'am. You will find His Highness awaiting your arrival with great anticipation."

"Very likely. Don't scowl so, Des. The prince will keep

129

the proprieties.'' She passed him on her way to change. Perhaps it was as well that Des would go along with her ladyship. Miss Quilling, who had gone over in Milsom Street to exchange a book for Hannah at Hookham's Library, would be shocked that she hadn't been included as Hannah's chaperone, but her sharp eyes were apt to observe more than Desmond ever saw.

Chapter Fourteen

Prince Andre went obediently into the kitchen in the wake of stout little Mrs. Plackett. From Hannah Jasper's attitude and her scarcely concealed amusement when she gave her orders, he had no doubt she believed this was his introduction to the life backstairs.

There is a deal about me, Miss Jasper, he thought, that you have yet to discover.

He was in his happiest mood in weeks.

There had been times when his waking nightmares were far worse than the fantasies of sleep. He had relived the sight of a vicious old man striking, even beating the fragile Eulalie. But when he approached Samson Croft the morning after the Waltzing Party, intending to demand the truth, warn him, beat the tough old rooster, or even kill him, it was Eulalie who saw him first, went into one of her infrequent tempers and raged that he must do nothing "to ruin matters."

He had only the vaguest notion of what that could mean, but his suspicions were aroused. Eulalie's ideas had always been highly complicated and involved. Was this another? Had she, perhaps, deliberately aroused her husband to violence in order to free herself from Old Samson in due time? The law was very clear. She would have no rights whatever.

But there might be monetary compensations if her husband's physical cruelty were made evident. Eulalie had always placed a high priority on money and the regal life of which she felt she had been cheated. He did not like it and tried to tell her so.

He had warned her that there must be no more deliberate attempts to arouse her husband's anger. She had laughed at that, though he could not imagine what humor she found in it. In the end, she had given him her promise, and as Prince Andre was leaving the Crescent, she started off to Yorkshire with her husband, petting and fondling him on the street as she was helped into Old Samson's huge traveling carriage.

So much was only to be expected of a bride, but she had given the departing prince such a significant grimace that he could only assume she was hoaxing Samson Croft. Not a very pretty picture.

During the days since Eulalie's departure he had found himself giving more and more thoughts to the young lady he had chosen to marry. He could not forget the refreshing excitement of holding her in his arms during the waltz, or the liveliness and playfulness of her disposition. She enjoyed their teasing encounters as much as he did. A rare young lady, Hannah Jasper.

Hannah. Definitely, that must be changed. There would also be a long period of training. He could imagine Hannah's quick indignation over the new person she must become as Princess of Bourbon-Valois. No matter. With her sense of humor and her resilience, as well as her dignity, she would make a success of life as his princess.

Mrs. Plackett apparently had no notion of his identity. Excellent. There were many moments, especially since he had met Miss Hannah Jasper, that he had wished he might always remain simply "Michael Meiggs, stable-groom." It was true that Miss Jasper had grown up in a rigidly bourgeois environment, with absurd restrictions in the conduct taken for granted a young female with monetary expectations, but he thought he might break that social barrier, so long as he appeared as Meiggs, the groom. Curiously enough, it was proving more difficult to break the social barrier with Hannah under his own identity as Andre-Charles-Louis de Bourbon-Valois, Prince of Bourbon-Valois.

He looked around the old-fashioned Jasper kitchen, where some foods were still prepared on the blackened hearth, and wished suddenly that he might change places with the real Michael Meiggs. He just might assure his happiness and that of his delightful quarry, Hannah Jasper.

Since little Mrs. Plackett put him forcibly in mind of endless sharp-spoken, softhearted cooks, housekeepers, and governesses of his youth, the prince had no difficulty in winning her over and very soon was eating one of the cook's fresh-baked currant scones while ensconced in what Mrs. Plackett called her "place of repose," an ancient armchair with badly worn cushions. It was so much like a throne that he had never felt more regal.

While chewing the scone he reflected on his future plans.

He had always been aware of his worth in the marriage mart. He could not recall a single young female of his close acquaintance, or, indeed, her elder sister, who hadn't thrown herself at his head in one way or another since he was twelve.

None except Hannah Jasper. He never knew for certain how he stood in her graces. Nor had he ever been sure. However, he had little doubt that he would prevail. His only conceivable rival appeared to be Miss Jasper's childhood friend Beaufort Croft, and, considering young Croft's dubious prospects and somewhat shady reputation, he seemed a more unlikely candidate than the equally debt-ridden Prince Andre.

It was therefore with considerable optimism that he considered the future. The important matter at hand was to win Hannah Jasper as his wife. A delightful challenge, during which he was able to do all the absurd things he had always wanted to do, such as carry on this masquerade, and with her full cooperation.

The young footman pushed the door open and stuck his

head in. "Miss waiting. She says the groom is to be quick about it."

The prince got up, made a sweeping bow to the cook and Mrs. Plackett, then followed the footman to the front of the house.

Miss Jasper stood in the foyer, smoothing gloves over her strong, thin fingers. Without ever having been a beauty, she seemed to have developed a style of her own. At the moment, in apricot muslin and an India shawl, with a chip straw hat sporting apricot ribbons to match, she presented an immensely vital and challenging picture.

She lashed one empty glove against her other hand.

"Meiggs, it is growing late." She looked at him, the laughing light in her eyes, and he bowed humbly.

"'Twas me fault entirely, Ma'am. Shall we be off?"

"Yes. We mustn't disappoint His Royal Highness. You know how impossible these foreign princes are. Forever standing on ceremony."

He agreed. "Even when they are princelings without country or throne. I do not see Sir Desmond and the lady. Will they be sharing my—ah—prince's barouche with us?"

The impish look was there again in her hazel eyes.

"No. Des is taking out his phaeton. I shall be riding in your barouche alone."

"Alone?"

"Naturally. You are the coachman; are you not?"

He laughed, realizing he hadn't quite pictured this difficulty in a coachman's life. He agreed ruefully.

"I had forgotten. I wonder, is it possible the Jasper coachman may be free to oblige? Then I might escort you properly. Inside the carriage."

"Oh, no. Poor man. He is beset by a severe attack of . . . of the gout. We never permit him to tool a carriage of any sort at this hour."

Having lost this little duel, he saluted the winning Miss Jasper and offered his arm. He watched with interest to see

134

if she would show any regret at being forced to ride alone while he rode up on the box.

Whatever her true feelings might be, she certainly revealed nothing but amusement to Prince Andre. She permitted him to help her into the elaborate open carriage, where she settled in lonely splendor, appearing to enjoy every moment of this unconventional drive. He swung up on the box, determined to make the best of things, but as he gathered up the reins from Sir Desmond's Jemie and set off for Everdene, he felt that he understood at last the man who first said: "hoist by one's own petard."

During the ride to Everdene, following for a short while the Bristol High Road, more or less toward the sun in the westerly sky, Prince Andre wondered what Miss Jasper was thinking as she rode alone behind him in the open barouche, which would have accommodated several others.

Prince Andre considered himself something of a whip, although for financial reasons, he had never allowed himself to be put up for the prestigious Four Horse Club; so it was with a further lowering of his self-esteem that he saw Captain Sir Desmond Jasper's team and phaeton dash by, with Lady Fiona seated beside the captain, holding her plumed hat with one hand and waving to Miss Jasper with the other. Wisely, she kept her "cruelly injured ankle" out of sight.

Prince Andre glanced over his shoulder to see Hannah Jasper with eyebrows raised in disapproval, though there was amusement in her eyes.

"Meiggs, I'm ashamed of you," she called to him. "My brother can be quite cowhanded at the reins, as you know very well. And yet, you have let him pass you."

No one had taken that tone with him since his first governess. He gritted his teeth to keep from replying that he would outjockey Master Desmond at the first straightaway but determined on the instant to give her a ride she would not soon forget. The springing of the team was only part of it.

Within a matter of a minute or two, the team was flying and His Highness was pushing them to still greater speed.

He expected every second to hear screams of indignation behind him, along with stern orders to desist. He would then pretend not to hear. Meanwhile, beneath the horses' hooves, the dust and pebbles flew, and the four wheels rattled and bumped over what the team failed to uproot.

Before the turn to Everdene he had come up hard on the Jasper phaeton, which was teetering along shakily. The prince had no doubt the unfortunate Lady Fiona was feeling the effects of seasickness by this time, but this was not his problem. He was still in momentary expectation of receiving a blow of some kind between his shoulders, and a warning to reduce speed.

The barouche rattled past Sir Desmond, sweeping a cloud of dust into his face and leaving him behind with his team badly blown.

Still nothing from Miss Jasper. Was she ill? Had she fainted? Puzzled and concerned, he glanced over his shoulder, only to find Hannah sitting back in reasonable comfort, with color in her cheeks, her hat somewhat blown but no less charming for that, and she was smiling.

"Very good, Meiggs. Someday, you must show me what you can do when you really give your team their heads. You might become a very tolerable whip."

He stared at her, feeling a fool, a reaction that would not be of much value in his future dealings with her. He made a conscious effort to grin back at her, recovered, saluted with his whip hand, and turned back to his team as the phaeton came rattling up behind him.

At a dead heat the two vehicles and their cargo reached the gates of Everdene, where they were welcomed by the real Meiggs, opening the double gates and calling, "You give them beasts quite a lathering, Highness. They'll be mighty glad of a gentle hand, so they will."

Prince Andre laughed and rode on. Meiggs strode up the straight avenue between rolling grassy slopes, in the wake of the barouche, while Des came up in perfect decorum with Lady Fiona in the phaeton.

Passing the reins to Meiggs at the steps, the prince leaped off the box quickly and was standing at the side of the barouche when Hannah Jasper got up to descend. She put out one hand, but since he was in a reckless mood, wanting very much to shock her, he raised both arms, closed them around either side of her body under her bosom, lifting her out and down to the steps, close against his body.

He had finally succeeded in disconcerting her. She stared up into his face, moistened her lips, and smiled. It was a curiously appealing smile, hesitant, as if she were unsure of her own charm. From their first encounter she had treated him like a man, not a prince. She challenged him at every turn, but lately, a new, intriguing dimension had been added. She excited him, as her body excited him now.

Then her brother—blast him!—appeared with Lady Fiona, who limped up the steps breathing hard, holding her hat with one hand, though the other still clutched Sir Desmond's arm.

His Highness let Miss Jasper slip through his hands. Hannah at once recovered her usual self-confidence. She reminded her brother, "We won, you know. By a hand's width. What a pity we didn't wager!"

Sir Desmond scowled in a friendly way. "Let me get Your Highness on a quarterdeck and we'll see who is master of the field."

"I agree, Captain." The prince offered his hand, which Sir Desmond took, bowing over it slightly but with none of the subservience of the prince's own people.

Meanwhile, lean, sedate Abercrombie, Prince Andre's highly efficient butler, came out to welcome these special visitors. DeVal, the prince's young valet, waited just inside the doors in the large, airy central hall. He said very little and was trying with some difficulty to extricate himself from the question of the prince's uninvited guest, Beau Croft. Beau's chief interest, as Prince Andre did not doubt, was the prince's invited guest Hannah Jasper.

Miss Jasper's reaction at sight of him annoyed the prince

far more than he would have thought. She took both Beau's hands in welcome.

"I haven't seen you this age, Beau. What on earth are you doing at Everdene?"

The sleek young man bent and kissed both her hands. It was too much, an overdone gesture the prince despised, because he recognized in himself a strong desire to repeat the tribute. Miss Jasper took the gesture lightly but with a warm look in her eyes that suggested an intimacy of years, the kind of close tie that had existed between Prince Andre and Princess Eulalie, made up of memories and the devotion of childhood.

But Eulalie is beyond my touch now, he thought. This fellow, on the other hand, could come between us if he dared.

Beau Croft explained smoothly, "Look upon me as the bearer of messages from on high, Hannah." He glanced around the group, smiling blandly, though his expression changed to puzzled amusement when he saw the prince's rough clothing.

Captain Jasper wanted to know what he meant by "on high," and Hannah cut in briskly, "Don't be tiresome, Beau. Say what you have to say."

"On high. The princess—that is to say, Mrs. Samson Croft—sent me."

Prince Andre looked at him with suspicion and anger. Eulalie must know this was a foolish thing to do, publicly opening up new communication between them and using as her messenger a troublemaker like Beau Croft, who was certain to spread the word. Worst of all, the prince was aware of the way Hannah Jasper suddenly raised her head and stared at him.

"Then Mr. and Mrs. Croft have returned from the north?" he asked, making the sound deliberately casual.

"Quite right, Highness. This noontime. Mrs. Croft and I, being in the nature of grandmother and grandson, the lady reposes confidence in me. She wanted you to know at once that they had returned."

For some reason as yet unknown to him, the prince found the return of Princess Eulalie troublesome. He could see that this news of her return disturbed Hannah Jasper, who said sharply, "Are you certain she arrived only at noon? Not earlier? Or last evening?"

"Absolutely, Hannah. I've only just seen their coach and four. Why?"

The prince watched her, puzzled. Hannah began, "Because someone has been . . ." She broke off, shrugged. "Another time." She turned away.

The delightful mood of Prince Andre's earlier encounter with Miss Jasper was rapidly fading, and he resented it, laying the blame directly upon this Beau Croft, who seemed to be so close in Miss Jasper's confidence. Worst of all, he had come to the point where he must become the prince again, and he hated it. His relations with Hannah had been disastrous in that role.

However, sooner or later, she must accept him as Andre-Charles-Louis, Prince de Bourbon-Valois. It might be as well to begin the transformation at once. He turned to Hannah. He couldn't resist taking up her hand and touching it to his lips while he looked into her eyes, hoping she read something of his feeling there. And more especially, that she realized he could be quite as gallant as her beloved Beau Croft!

Perhaps she did. She smiled, though she was clearly conscious of everyone's attention. She knew then that they were all waiting to see if she would fall under his blandishments and let herself become Princess de Bourbon-Valois.

"Forgive me. I cannot very well play the host in these dusty rags. Lady Fiona, Abercrombie, please make my guests comfortable. DeVal, come with me."

Almost at once he wished he need not leave Miss Jasper with her old and much too intimate friend, young Croft. He must rely upon Lady Fiona to prevent any tête-à-tête between them. He noted, however, that his valet also seemed interested in the party left in the gold withdrawing room.

That was odd. DeVal seldom let his curiosity get the better of him.

When they reached his dressing room and DeVal was laying out a more respectable and princely wardrobe, the prince looked hard at him and said, "Come. Out with it. You disapprove of all my masquerading, don't you?"

The valet said coolly, "It is not my place to approve or disapprove, Sir. I am aware of the severity of Your Highness's needs."

"Damned if you are!" The prince was not at all pleased with this plain speaking. "Am I to understand my servants are discussing my debts? Next, they will be moaning over the price I pay for my claret, not to mention forbidding me to furnish champagne for my guests."

The valet removed the soiled towel His Highness had used on his dusty hands. "Not in my presence, Sir. And certainly not champagne."

With DeVal's help the prince dressed in silence, asking after a few moments of irritated silence, "And why is champagne sacrosanct, may I ask?"

DeVal gave him a quick look, as if analyzing his real thoughts. "That would seem to be obvious, Sir. And quite beyond discussion."

His Highness tossed aside a cravat whose creases he had spoiled in his impatience and irritability at this conversation. DeVal handed him another. The prince studied DeVal's dark eyes in the mirror.

"What the devil is this all about? Why should champagne be beyond discussion?"

Avoiding what began to seem a dangerous subject, DeVal offered him a third cravat of equally pristine white, stainless and uncreased. But by this time the prince had become highly suspicious.

"Well? Damn, speak up!"

"The . . . the lady, Sir. I mean, the lady's problem . . . with—with—" Belatedly, DeVal realized that his master did not know he was talking about. To avoid the painful disclosure, DeVal brought out another cravat. The prince, having arranged the second cravat to his satisfaction, took the new one, crumpled it up angrily, and threw it into a corner. The valet winced and went to pick it up, caressing the soft material more or less unconsciously between his fingers.

"I collect you are talking about Miss Jasper." Without waiting for an answer, the prince went on grimly, "The lady who will soon be Princess of Bourbon-Valois."

This brought an anguished, "Oh, Your Highness!" But DeVal caught himself quickly. "Sir, it has been done before. My own uncle. As stiff a drinker as ever drained a mug. But he married a Methodist and it was the end of him. Of his taste for claret, that is to say, Sir."

Prince Andre knew quite well that if he raised a greater scene over these preposterous rumors it would soon spread through the household, and from here to God knows where, so he gave the matter a forced laugh and assured DeVal, "You have been imposed upon, my dear fellow. Someone has made you a figure of fun. Miss Jasper has a modest and quite respectable taste for champagne. The gin story was equally false. It came about as the result of an accident. Two gentlemen leaving the White Hart, one carrying a mug of gin on a wager. That is all."

He added on leaving the room, "I take it you had the story from Hoog. General Hoogstratten. You must know he can be depended on for the most preposterous gossip."

"No, Sir. It—"

"If he continues, he will soon find he has left this house, and any other where I reside."

"Yes, Sir." DeVal looked suitably shocked at the storm he had weathered.

Prince Andre went down the stairs, more concerned over the discussion than he wanted known. He was well aware that such senseless yet malicious gossip could ruin Hannah Jasper's standing in the tight little world of Bath society. It could even travel to London.

Such stories could cause her endless embarrassment and humiliation if his connections in Britain or on the Continent attacked her for marrying a man in his position. Miss Jasper was far too proud to make her vows if reminded by one and all that the Princess of Bourbon-Valois must not be a subject for gossip.

Somewhat to his surprise, he realized as he entered the ground floor that he had an even more powerful reason for protecting her from scandal. He wanted to spend his life with her. If she were forced or persuaded to cry off, his personal loss would be greater than any monetary problems. He would never find another minx so unpredictable and enchanting, so self-sufficient and charming, so exactly the life companion he wanted and needed.

Damn the scandalmongers!

He came into the big withdrawing room just as Hannah and Beau Croft brought their glasses together in a toast. Hannah and that fellow were nearly as close as their glasses. They both drank, emptying their glasses and laughing. What the deuce was so amusing?

Chapter Fifteen

Beau Croft studied his empty glass and then Hannah's, remarking as he pointed to her glass, "I cannot ask for a better birthday toast than that. You emptied the glass, my girl. You've a good head for it."

Hannah laughed. "Fortunately, your birthday comes only once a year. I do not engage to empty a glass so quickly every day, wager or no. By the by, you owe me a guinea."

"Ho, you'll never see that, Hannah," Des called from the terrace windows across the room where Lady Fiona was pointing out to him the bowling green and the stables.

"On the contrary." Beau reached into the little slit pocket where he carried his watch and an elaborate fob. "Behold. I pay my debts. And it was worth it to see you empty the glass at a blow, so to speak."

Hannah set down her own glass, accepted the coin, and turned to find her reticule where she had dropped it on the rosewood sofa table. As she did so she saw that the elegantly paneled double doors were open from the wide entrance hall and Prince Andre stood there watching Hannah and Beau. He looked breathtaking in the theatrical white uniform of a pre-revolutionary French officer that he had worn so briefly on her last visit to Everdene.

He also looked angry. She wondered if he could possibly be jealous of Beau's attention to her. Probably she flattered herself. Looking as he did, and with his ancient titles to boot, he was unlikely to find Miss Hannah Jasper so irresistible that his jealousy was aroused.

Very likely he feared that Beau would win the Jasper fortune or, at all events, the considerable share that remained at Hannah's disposal. Hardened in her determination by this reminder, she smiled sweetly, even bobbing a slight curtsy.

"Your Highness, you are in time to toast Mr. Croft. This is his birthday."

The prince's flickering smile was hardly warm. "Congratulations, Mr. Croft. May we know the year? Thirty? Thirty-two?"

Beau swallowed hard, also swallowing whatever resentment he felt. "Twenty-seven, Sir."

Hannah watched them with amusement. Even Des came across the salon guffawing. "Well, Beau, that should teach you to linger over the gaming tables all night! What do you say, Highness? Shall we empty a glass to old Beau? I think we owe it to him. Lord, to be thought thirty when one is so much younger! I recall those days very well." He shuddered elaborately.

To Hannah's surprise the prince said stiffly, "I myself will be thirty in three months." No one said a thing. He stepped into the room. "Where is Abercrombie? Or a maid? Never mind." He went to the sideboard, poured champagne into two glasses, and set back the now empty bottle. "Mr. Croft, your very good health."

Beau took the other glass, tipped it slightly in His Highness's direction, and began to drink.

Somewhat to Hannah's surprise, the prince set his own glass down and with unexpected good humor signaled to Lady Fiona. "Mr. Croft is our guest, my lady. Will you be good enough to show him the family collection of brasses and rapiers? Oh, and the new Waterford china."

"Waterford glasses, Sir."

The prince was undisturbed by his mistake. "Yes. That too. I am persuaded Sir Desmond will also find them fascinating."

Des asked Hannah a question with his tawny eyebrows. She nodded. He grinned and took Lady Fiona's hand. Beau was less easy to satisfy. Hannah was amused at his useless effort to keep from being ensnared by the prince. Within minutes Lady Fiona was leading the two men through the long salon with its many mahogany and rosewood furnishings, so specially marked by brass and leather insets.

Meanwhile, His Highness rather neatly cornered Hannah and maneuvered her out onto the terrace, down the three steps, and into the uneven dirt path between rows of the kitchen garden. During the time she allowed herself to be separated from all her respectable chaperons, Hannah had been cynically amused by these efforts on the part of two men who—she made no doubt—were thinking very much about her fortune and very little about herself.

It was a lowering reflection, her only satisfaction being her awareness of their motives, which provided her with an impregnable defense.

She was thinking this when she became aware that His Highness seemed to be spending considerable time on a description of the bowling green, the fields, the seasonal beauty of Everdene, the stables with their much admired team of "Valois Blacks."

She wondered what interest he fancied all this would hold for her and suddenly realized he was about to offer for her.

"If you were not so very much your own woman," he told her, "I would speak to your brother first. But . . ."

That did make her laugh. "Poor Des! He certainly would not know how to reply. He is the dearest of brothers, but he hasn't the least notion what my feelings are, upon any subject."

He smiled. His fingers had tightened over her hand, and when she tried surreptitiously to release herself she found it impossible to break from him. Why must he look like that, like all the heroes of all the romances she obtained from Hookham's Library? If only his motives were less transparent!

"Nevertheless, I believe these matters, settlements, rights, and the rest, must be put in the hands of others more versed in legal affairs. I myself haven't the remotest idea of how to proceed." He saw the beginnings of a frown narrow her eyes and he asked after an anxious instant, "You have said yes, haven't you?"

She did not know why she should be so stunned. Surely his conversation had indicated a proposal. She looked up at him, wishing with all her heart that when she said yes, she might actually possess his love. The truth was so different, so ugly.

His Highness was only behaving in the manner expected of her class and his. He did nothing outrageous or insulting in marrying her for her fortune, yet she hated his action and his proposal, because she wanted so much more of him.

"Miss Jasper . . . Hannah. What is it to be?"

The hurt was deep. She wanted to wound him in the only way she could. First, an acceptance. Later, when he counted upon her fortune, would come the real blow. She would cry off. She gave him a glittering smile.

"You flatter me, Sir."

"Then you accept?" His relief was palpable. His sensuous fingers ran along the bridge of her nose to her mouth and she thrilled to his touch. He bent his head and kissed her on the lips. She hesitated, partly from shock. No man had ever taken such liberties without her permission. But her own response overpowered her instincts, and she returned his kiss, touching his mouth, which had intrigued her so long, her lips clinging to his until a sound somewhere, a window closing, brought her back to an awareness of the proprieties. She found it less easy to release herself.

"Please. You must know I would be ruined if we were seen like this."

"Even though you are to be my wife?"

"Especially so, Your Highness. All such actions are acceptable only among securely married persons."

146

"And not even then in public," he teased. "Oh, you Anglo-Saxons!"

She laughed but would not let him touch her as they returned to the Hall. They were souls of propriety when Lady Fiona and her escorts saw them, although Hannah did not miss the tension in Beau Croft's slender form when he saw them together.

Hannah's cynicism was complete. Doubtless Beau feared she would no longer lend him money when she became Princess de Bourbon-Valois.

Absurd thought. Almost as if she truly intended to oblige His Highness with her hand and her money.

It was the prince who made the announcement to Desmond while Hannah stood by looking demure and pretending to ignore Beau Croft's frowns, scowls, and attempts to catch her eye.

"Sir Desmond," the prince said on a flattering note of pride, "may I speak to you privately on a matter concerning your sister?"

Des looked surprised and made no effort to hide the true state of affairs. "No use, dear fellow. No use at all. Hannah is her own mistress. If she's taken a fancy to have you, you won't need my consent. Not but what you have it, to be sure."

Lady Fiona Westerby laughed behind her fan. Hannah was amused, but Beau actually lost color and His Highness was somewhat taken aback.

"Well, then, thank you very much. You have made me the happiest of men." He extended one hand to Des, who wrung it heartily.

"My pleasure entirely, old—that is, Sir."

Beau moved to Hannah's side, muttering, "You know why he offers. You can't be serious."

"Of course I can't be," she whispered. "Be quiet."

His troubled expression lifted, and he began to watch the celebration with speculative interest.

While Des rambled on about his hopes for his sister's

happiness under the beaming smile of Lady Fiona, Beau interrupted boisterously, "But shall there not be toasts to this royal match? Pardon, Your Highness. May I be permitted to propose a toast?"

"By all means." Prince Andre made a sweeping gesture toward the bellpull behind Beau, who at once rang for Abercrombie. When the butler arrived and glasses were refilled, Hannah was surprised that His Highness refused glasses for himself and Hannah. With his arm around her he boasted, "We have no need of champagne, Miss Jasper and I. We shall make our own happiness."

Beau was stopped with his arm extended and the glass at Hannah's fingertips. He did not usually look so embarrassed.

"Oh. I beg pardon. But I thought . . . only a few sips . . . Shouldn't be any harm in . . ." He stared down at the glass, then at Hannah and back again. "However, I daresay you are right." He withdrew the glass and set it down untouched.

It was enough. Hannah understood very well what these detestible men were telling her. Obviously, they believed the gossip about her shocking taste for wine and spirits. With a great ef ort she managed to conceal her hurt and humiliation with a smiling agreement that wavered but did not fail her.

"His Highness speaks for me. Our happiness needs no wine."

Lady Fiona suggested that a small dinner party might be a more appropriate celebration and, she added, "give us the chance to discuss the future role of Her Highness, the Princess"—She hesitated, glanced around helplessly—"Princess Hannah?"

The prince asked with a too casual air, "What are your other Christian names, *cherie*?"

Hannah gritted her teeth. "Agatha."

A deathlike hush fell upon the group. Hannah saved the awkward moment. "But in any case, we cannot remain. Sir

Desmond and I are entertaining at a dinner for a few friends.''

Des raised his head, opened his mouth, but merely cleared his throat.

In the end, this moment, which Hannah had always looked forward to with romantic eyes, the time of her betrothal, proved anticlimactic. She let His Highness kiss her hand, lingering with it in his fingers while he looked at her lips.

"I wish you would let me escort you home."

"Thank you, Sir. But my brother will be quite sufficient."

He looked as if he might kiss her lips, a sight that would have been seen and gossiped about throughout Bath before the night was over, but he refrained. He insisted on helping her into her brother's phaeton, and she hadn't the will to resist when his hand closed around her slender waist and he raised her into the high, fragile seat, reminding her, "If only the groom, Meiggs, might carry you home."

"By all means," she teased, with her eyes sparkling at the memory. "Please call him. I see him down at the gatehouse."

He laughed in response and the old camaraderie, the easy, jesting familiarity, seemed to be restored between them. Before letting her go, he kissed her gloved fingertips again and then stood watching as Des gave his team the office to start. The phaeton went rattling along toward the gates of the estate. Hannah looked back and waved, telling herself there was no harm in enjoying these moments.

Des chuckled, the sound startling her out of her dream of what never could be. "Fancy having to call you Your Highness."

"What fustian!"

He looked at her, frowning a little. "Seems only fitting. You will be a princess. Princess Hannah." His chuckle became a guffaw, which she didn't appreciate.

"I wish you would not talk about it. Nothing is agreed

149

upon, and you may believe me when I say nothing will be done . . . Not when they discover I have scarcely two thousand a year of income.''

This time he did stare. ''Dear old girl! You've an income upwards of twenty thousand. More than mine by several thousand. Unless you've been dipping mighty deep.''

She hesitated. She did not like to keep secrets from her brother, whom she loved more than anyone else in the world, but Des was an innocent who understood few, if any, complexities of human nature. When there were secrets swirling around his splendid head, he was uncomfortable and insisted at once that he wanted no part of them.

Rapidly, she sorted out what she wanted Desmond to know. ''I never gamble. But I have reinvested nearly all my income in the Funds as well as sugar and coffee plantations in Jamaica.''

''Hot country, Jamaica. All the Indies, come to that. But good Lord, old girl, two thousand a year! Your prince isn't going to marry for two thousand.''

''No,'' she admitted, feeling the hurt more strongly than ever. ''He can scarcely support Everdene Hall on two thousand a year.''

It was a lowering reflection.

Des would have continued on this line, but they had come out upon the High Road and he was forced to attend his team before they tangled with a high-stepping team of grays heading toward Bristol.

Hannah remained silent, considering her best plan of campaign in what might prove to be a more painful revenge than she had anticipated.

She was glad to reach Queen Square and her normal life behind those walls, only to find Miss Quilling awaiting the Jaspers with a message for Des.

''It seems Hannah isn't the only member of the family who is pursued by royalty. Master Desmond, a Croft lackey brought this epistle. I sincerely trust it is from Mr. Samson Croft.''

Des chucked her under the chin. "I'll wager it is more Hannah's matter than mine. Old Samson has always had a fancy for my little sister. Once fed her ginger moogin." All the same, he took the folded and sealed sheet from Miss Quilling and studied it intently. Miss Quilling and Hannah exchanged glances.

Much as they would have given to know the contents of that missive, neither woman was allowed to do so. Sir Desmond retired to his own quarters, where, his valet confided later to Miss Quilling's niece, Kitty, "The captain reads and rereads, as if it were an Admiralty Order."

In Hannah's presence Miss Quilling asked, "What is his reaction?"

Kitty said brightly to Hannah, "Oh, Mum, he's ever so cross. He paces the floor and cuffs his fist into his palm right cross-like."

Hannah murmured, "It doesn't sound well. What can he be about?"

"Who, Mum?" Kitty wanted to know.

Miss Quilling shooed her out of the room. "Never you mind, girl. Go back and see what you can discover. But be discreet."

With the maid gone Miss Quilling asked, "How can this princess creature make Master Des angry? He scarcely knows her."

"I'm very much afraid she practices the same trick upon His Highness and upon Des. Something to do with her mistreatment by Mr. Croft. I don't believe it."

"Well, he was never a sweet goer, as they say. But I do not recall hearing that he ever raised a hand against a female. Still, some women do drive a man to it, I daresay."

"Rubbish. If His Highness believes the woman's tales, he is a great fool. And Des is a greater fool."

"What's this?" a very masculine voice demanded outside Hannah's bed-sitting room as Des looked in at them. "I may be a fool, but who is my lesser rival?"

Miss Quilling said quickly, "Now, Master Des, you know your sister's funning ways. She meant nothing."

Hannah ruined her efforts. "I meant everything, Des. If you believe Mrs. Croft is ill treated, you are sadly mistaken."

"And you, of course, are never mistaken." Des lumbered into the room, his big face like a thundercloud. "If you are speaking of that sainted little lady who has endured God knows what horrors, you are very much in error. I have seen the ghastly evidence."

"Really, Des, how can you believe such fustian? I have Mr. Croft's own word that the woman is clumsy. She has several times injured herself. Perhaps she doesn't wish anyone to guess at her clumsiness."

"Because Old Samson tells you?" He brought his fist down on the satin-puffed back of the chaise longue in his wrath. The couch shivered under his force. "You believe that ogre, but you fail to credit those who are truly your friends."

Hannah stared. "And who might these friends be?"

"Her Highness especially. It was she who defended you, my girl."

Hannah began to laugh. There was more contempt than pleasure in the sound. "I was not aware that I needed a defense."

Des twisted the satin under his hand. His thunderous look had dissolved into something rather more sullen and shamed.

"A deal of rubbish. Lord knows how it got about. That day when you were at the White Hart Inn and Tavern. Then the business in the Abbey Yard near the Pump Room. And something about your drinking too much champagne at the Crofts' waltzing party. At all events, we heard it discussed that evening and Her Highness denied it. Indignantly."

"Who discussed it?"

"Good Lord! Beg pardon, Quilly, I've no notion. Some friends of the Crofts and that stout fellow, General Hoog

. . . something. Matter of fact, the general is the closest confidant of your noble betrothed.''

''I know him,'' she said slowly, remembering the day of the ''Blue Ruin'' episode and the obvious disbelief in the face of General Hoogstratten.

''Well, then.'' Des shrugged, pulled himself together. ''Your prince seems to want you, despite the gossip, which shows the fellow is superior to most of the royal princelings hanging out for a fortune.'' He started out of the room but stopped in the doorway with a last thoughtful bit of advice. ''However, I shouldn't keep to that tale about two thousand a year, if I were you.''

Miss Quilling gasped, ''Two thousand! My dear, who would believe that?''

Hannah said very lightly, ''I shouldn't wonder if Des is right. I am hardly worth taking, with only two thousand annually.''

Chapter Sixteen

His Highness was out on his property, trying to view it with the eyes of his betrothed, when Lady Fiona Westerby crossed the kitchen garden and followed the wheel-rutted path that wound around the west face of the Hall toward the stables. Meiggs was with the prince, evidently trying to persuade him that Miss Hannah Jasper would prize his stables more than the rich green fields and the countryside.

Lady Fiona gave a sketch of a curtsy upon the prince's nod, but she rushed to say, "I shouldn't be surprised if Meiggs is right, Sir. One might almost say it was Your Highness's ability with horses that first attracted the young lady."

That brought a smile. The prince wondered how much she knew of his masquerade, but he had to admit she was right. From the moment of their first meeting, he and Hannah had known their happiest moments around horses.

"Did you wish to speak to me, Fiona?"

"A lady to see Your Highness."

"Miss Jasper. She must see the sweet-going filly we've added, Meiggs. She will appreciate the little beauty." He gave over the reins of his own favorite black mare to Meiggs after one last friendly slap at the mare's hindquarter.

He started back to the house with Lady Fiona, who explained in an expressionless voice, "Not Miss Jasper, Sir. Mrs. Croft and her maid."

"Oh." He stopped on the path, frowning. "That was unwise. She will have half of Bath gossiping about her if she does not take care."

"Yes, Sir. And Clotilde, the abigail, has a great fondness for trinkets." Lady Fiona added after a slight pause, "Even Yorkshire trinkets. She may be reporting to Mr. Croft."

The prince looked at her curiously. "You have no liking for Her Highness, have you?"

"I think, Sir, that she finds it too easy to forget she is a wife and no longer—forgive me, Sir—no longer your betrothed."

She eyed him in an uneasy way, but he tried not to be angered by the truth, though his first inclination, built by habit, was to defend his Eulalie. The truth was, she had ceased to be "his" Eulalie when she had married Samson Croft, nor could he acquit her of marrying the old man's riches.

His chief concern now was that Hannah might hear of Eulalie's heedless conduct in visiting a single man at his home, as though it were an assignation.

"It was a very foolish thing to do," he agreed, to Lady Fiona's relief. "But you know Her Highness. She is used to having her way in all things."

"Yes, Sir. I do know."

He did not answer that. Annoyingly enough, Eulalie compounded her unwise conduct by boldly walking out on the terrace, touching her fingers to her lips, and waving her hand at him, very much as though they were still lovers. She seemed unaware that Meiggs or Lady Fiona or any unseen servant of the Hall might spread gossip about her conduct.

"My dearest," she greeted the prince as he joined her. She took his hands. He was further annoyed by this deliberate flouting of the conventions. He found himself comparing her conduct with that of his Hannah, who had flouted a few conventions when she flirted with "the stable-groom." But that was quite different. Then too, it was Hannah, and he grinned at the memory of those delightful moments with her.

Eulalie commended him roguishly for that smile. "You see? You cannot be cross with me. I am persuaded you were thinking that very thing this minute."

"Would you hazard a wager on that?" But his irony was lost on her. She still held his hands. He raised one of her hands to his lips, then released both hands. He was conscious of a vagrant thought quite new to him as her rejected fingers clawed into her palms. Those delicate hands could be very grasping at times.

She looked around, evidently finding too great an audience for a personal scene, nipped at his sleeve, whispering urgently, "My darling, we must talk, you and I. It has been forever since we were truly alone. Come."

"Do you care so little about your reputation?" he asked, but he walked across the terrace with her and into the long reception salon where the princess's abigail, a plump little brunette with lively eyes, watched their every move. Something about the girl's intense fascination with them made him suspect that Lady Fiona was right. She might be in Samson Croft's pay.

He gave Eulalie a low-voiced reminder of this, but she tossed her head, the curling blue feather of her bonnet tickling him. He avoided the feather thereafter.

"Andre, he will not trouble us long. I came to tell—to remind you." There was a new urgency in her voice, that voice he had always likened to charming golden bells.

He forgot the maid, who had been straining so hard to hear their conversation that she had now eased her way half the length of the salon and was leaning on a sideboard to hear better.

"He is a strong, healthy fellow, and I do not wish him ill."

"Nor I, dearest. But his conduct to me has shocked all our acquaintances. My husband makes another enemy every time he strikes—but I need not mention such matters. You understand." She ran the fingers of one hand over the other wrist, then touched the fading bruises over her throat, not quite concealed by the ruffled neckline of her jonquil silk afternoon gown.

He had winced at the sight of them on former occasions, almost ready to kill the brutal old man who had done this thing. But today he saw her tight, triumphant smile and for the first time was repulsed by more than the sight of such cruelty.

"I hope I misunderstand you, Lalie. But I wonder how far you would go to destroy that old man."

"I?" She was indignant. "Do you imagine I would destroy my husband? If he behaves so brutally, he must expect to reap the harvest. Must he not?"

"I wonder." Suspicion took fresh root. He took her wrist suddenly, the unscarred wrist. She pouted.

"You hurt me."

"Even as a child you bruised easily. In your play you bruised yourself, I remember."

"But by accident, Andre." The quickness with which she said this increased his suspicion.

He let her hand go. "I did nothing to that wrist. There was no brutality. Would you use that wrist against me and say I had done it deliberately to hurt you?"

She looked down, biting her lip. "Did you?" She added, "Of course not."

"Yet I've no doubt it will be black and blue tonight."

She stamped her foot angrily. "You still do not understand. It is for you. I knew I must act quickly. There was talk that you would actually marry that bourgeoise. A dreadful, drinking creature whose grandfather was a tenant farmer."

With a curious lack of feeling he thought that she had never looked more beautiful, dainty, feminine, all golden light, including the sharp, hard light in her blue eyes. Most astonishing to him was his own indifference to her beauty.

Where had it gone, that boyish adoration of her selfish but enchanting ways? He had matured late.

"I must tell you, I intend to marry that bourgeoise."

She beat her hands together in her anxious effort to sway him. "It is her fortune. I know that. Give me time. I will have a fortune. Only a little time, darling."

He saw no reason to continue this argument, which must be the most humiliating of her life. He moved her aside, motioned to the abigail. "Mrs. Croft is leaving. Please give her your arm. This summer heat is too much for her. Take care."

Eulalie looked stricken. He was sorry. He knew he should feel more than this pity, but he could not forget the cutting, derogatory way in which Eulalie had referred to Hannah Jasper. Hannah had done nothing to earn this contempt. He resented it for himself but was rapidly learning to resent it for someone he loved.

"Very well, darling. You will see how obedient I can be. I shall leave you. But I may expect to see you at the concert in the Upper Rooms tomorrow night?"

His smile was tinged with sarcasm. "Mr. Samson Croft does not appear to me a lover of concerts."

"Don't be difficult. He must accompany me. I shall see to it. As a matter of fact, it is absolutely necessary that he should accompany me. And you?"

"Like your husband, I will be dragged to the concert out of devotion."

"Ah. Sweetly spoken."

"To my betrothed."

Her smile flickered briefly, then was restored in all its winning splendor. "Dear Andre. I know you too well to let you hurt me. Good-bye. Until tomorrow night."

He saw Eulalie and her maid off in the old Croft landaulet whose coachman, footman, and team waited patiently outside the front steps of the hall.

Eulalie looked back, waving with her mischievous tight smile, until His Highness turned and went into the hall.

On the night of the next Assembly Rooms concert, Desmond seemed in such excellent spirits at the prospect of a concert featuring the music of Monteverdi and Franchetti, who were total strangers to him, that Hannah suspected his real interests lay elsewhere. She only hoped they did not lie with Samson Croft's wife. She was forever hearing gossip about the cruelty of old Samson toward his wife and still refused to believe it.

Hannah herself felt that she looked her best in glittering white splendor, from crescent diadem in her chestnut curls to her white satin slippers. She seldom wore the diamond set, which had belonged to her mother, and she told herself she wore it now only to lead Prince Andre to his fall when he discovered her immediate fortune was nonexistent. But because she was reasonably honest with herself, she knew she wanted to look her best in the prince's eyes, so that she might be at least a minor threat to the much discussed beauty of Eulalie Croft.

As they were approaching the New Assembly Rooms and encountered Colonel Forbin, Des revealed his true interest in the concert. "I trust we aren't about to see more of that old ogre's work, I can tell you. For sixpence I'd call the fellow out. They say that fragile little creature is in constant danger from him."

"You mustn't believe all the tiresome gossip you hear," Hannah reminded him.

Colonel Forbin came to her support in a backhanded way. "Indeed not, old fellow. Look at all the disgusting talk about Miss Jasper. Lies, yes. But I myself have been forced to chastise at least two gossipmongers."

"What? Am I now said to be committing fresh crimes against the order of things?"

"Infamous!" the colonel went on. "As though you had ever been—been—"

"Drunk?"

"Infamous!"

Hannah pretended a nonchalance she was far from feeling. "Where have I been drinking now?"

The colonel said uncomfortably, "Servants' gossip. Something about a celebration of Beaufort Croft's birthday. Ridiculous, naturally. I gave the fellow a facer, I can tell you. Bruised my knuckles. It's my belief young Croft is spreading these tales in order to win your hand. He's under the hatches, or will be, shortly. He must marry wealth. Never liked the fellow myself."

Strange, Hannah thought, before I met Prince Andre I had supposed I would marry Beau someday.

She turned from that thought quickly. There was little likelihood she would marry either man, unless one of them was willing to take her with a mere two thousand in income. Even then, she knew she could never marry Beau. Not since she had discovered what painful joy there was in a real and passionate love.

Well, I've admitted it to myself, she realized. I love Andre-Charles-Louis de Bourbon-Valois, and much good it may do me! Unless I buy him, and that I refuse to do.

As they entered the Assembly Rooms and were approached by their friends, it seemed to Hannah that there was a perceptible difference in the attitude toward her. Hannah sensed that the whispers she could not quite hear were about her, and she caught several sly glances among the young ladies who had formerly been her admirers. The young beaux of her past, with whom she often flirted, were more circumspect. She was not greatly comforted when she discovered the gossipy interest in her was excited by rumors of her impending betrothal and not of her supposed drinking proclivities.

"Tell me, do, Miss Jasper," Clarissa Tremoyle begged. "Is it true you are to be a princess? Must we all kneel to you? Will you wear a crown and sit on a throne?"

"None of those things. Don't be nonsensical." She wished very much that she hadn't let things go so far, even to embarrass His Highness.

"But General Hoogstratten says you must learn ever so many things, to be worthy. To be the prince's bride, I mean."

Hannah cut away this ground. "General Hoogstratten knows nothing of the matter, I assure you. I regard a free Englishwoman as the equal of any prince."

Clarissa clapped her hands and then pointed to the great chandelier overhead. "How like a queen you look, with those crystal lusters gleaming on your hair! It needs but a coronet to complete the portrait."

This compliment, however, was somewhat dimmed by a disturbance at the opposite end of the salon, and Miss Tremoyle joined the enthusiasm with which several other persons in the Octagon Room turned to fawn over Mrs. Samson Croft. The princess, having settled her husband in a large milord chair, smiled wistfully upon the group that began to surround her.

Hannah nodded and returned the princess's greeting but was not surprised at the little gasp that went up when the others saw Eulalie Croft's pretty face. Even the tawny wisp of curl that dangled over one cheek did not disguise the reddened mark, almost a rope burn, across the left side of her jaw.

Hannah glanced at Samson Croft in his chair across the formal room. The old man's eyes looked hooded, but he seemed to be studying her. To Hannah's surprise he motioned to her with one forefinger. An instant later his valet brought him a glass of something that appeared to be water but was probably gin. He drank quickly, as if it were water.

There was no way to approach him now without arousing endless gossip. Also, rather late in the day, it occurred to her that Samson Croft was looking very grim, quite able to inflict those bruises on his bride. In that event, Eulalie Croft was a badly wronged woman, and Hannah herself had contributed to that wrong. She was shamed by this reflection and began to suspect the woman might be innocent of spreading the lies about Hannah's drinking.

Could it all be a coincidence, the natural mischief of a few people who loved to gossip?

Those who had subscribed to the concert were making their way through the salons to the chairs in the long music room. Hannah found herself urged to join George Forbin in one set of chairs and Beau Croft in another. Since there were unsettled matters between Beau and her, she accepted his invitation, swept up the end of her satin and lace train over her hand and rested her other hand on Beau Croft's figured silk sleeve.

She began at once, "Beau, why do you think these stories have begun?"

Beau was looking drawn and tired. His temper seemed very uneven, ready for a quick explosion.

"I've no doubt the evidence goes before her. Anyone may see it."

She stared at him. "What can you mean? Since it is a lie, I scarcely see how it goes before me, as you say."

Beau laughed, a sudden burst of sound. "You? I'm speaking of my damnable new grandmama and her wounds of war."

He too could be surprising. She joined his laughter. "I thought you had fallen victim to her charms."

"All to a purpose, Hannah. I think you know what purpose that is."

"The fortune of Hannah Jasper?" she goaded him lightly.

He studied her fingers on his arm. "Think what you like. My feelings will not change, no matter what I do. Remember that. They were rooted too long ago." He frowned. The dark pessimism masked his face again. "Hannah, he is a shallow, greedy foreigner. You know nothing about him, about his nature. About the man."

"And I know everything about you."

He hesitated. "Not quite everything. But in the end, I promise you, you will see that we are suited."

They were about to enter the music salon when a disturbance behind them made Beau turn and swear at what he saw. Hannah was startled by his vehemence but suspected the reason for his annoyance.

Prince Andre had arrived with his entourage, General Hoogstratten, fawning and fluttering as much as anyone his size could flutter, and Lady Fiona Westerby, whose attention was upon Desmond. Desmond, unfortunately, had just seen little Eulalie Croft and hurried to join her, crossing in front of the prince's party to do so. He was stopped by Her Ladyship's voice. Good manners made him linger to exchange pleasantries with her.

Hannah became aware of a quickened heartbeat at sight of the prince. He was in evening dress, like the followers of Beau Brummel, all stark black with snowy white linen, and, most exciting, he made it clear to those watchful eyes that he was seeking only Hannah Jasper. She smiled but did not move from Beau's side in the doorway to the music salon. A rustling within that crowded room told her that numerous musical guests had risen in order to stare at the prince. Or perhaps, she thought uncomfortably, at the meeting between His Royal Highness and the lady rumor assigned as his future wife.

Not for the first time, she wished with all her heart that their expectations might be hers.

Beau cut sharply into her dreams. "Shall we take our seats?"

Before she could decide which choice to make, His Highness was in front of her, his eyes looking warmly into hers as he took up her free hand, kissing the small area of flesh where her glove fastened.

"Miss Jasper, may I say you look enchanting, precisely like a fairy tale princess."

Hannah knew that in the dawn light beyond the influence of diamonds, crystal lusters and the prince's excellent mood, Hannah would look as she had always looked, a reasonably attractive young woman much praised for "charm" and "a frank, honest quality" that was called "delightful." But tonight she noted proudly upon catching sight of herself in the long pier-glass at home, that she looked dazzling enough for the extravagant label of beauty.

"Thank you. Your Highness is gracious." She made her curtsy, wondering if, as his wife, she might be made to curtsy in their private moments.

But, of course, they were not going to be married. She must bear that in mind.

Meanwhile, as he examined her from head to foot, Prince Andre pleased her by doing so without his quizzing glass. She rewarded him with a smile that lighted her hazel eyes and evidently pleased him more, for he asked if he might escort her into the concert. She explained, trying not to show her disappointment, "I am being escorted by Mr. Croft, Sir."

The two men exchanged cool greetings, with the prince showing indifference and Beau a sense of quiet triumph.

Hannah suggested, to her own surprise, "A lady has two sides, Your Highness."

The prince smilingly agreed, and to Beau's marked displeasure, he followed them into the room, finding a gilt chair on Hannah's left. To make a bad matter worse, from Beau's viewpoint, His Highness began to converse with Hannah in low, intimate tones interspersed with the laughter of private enjoyment.

Hannah, who genuinely liked Franchetti's operas, found herself spending most of the next hour exchanging pleasantries with the prince, who was in a delightful mood, full of optimistic plans for a future he assumed they would share. She teased him for some time, trying to accept his plans as a form of humor.

"A honeymoon on the Continent, visiting every bit of ground that was once a part of the Valois heritage. Fancy! This will be the first time English travelers have been welcomed in Europe since the Revolution, if we except that abortive business in 1802.''

''There are no limits to the possibilities,'' she agreed on a sardonic note. ''Moscow, Far Cathay, exotic Samarkand? Where, precisely, is Samarkand, by the by?''

''I have made purchase of a filly you must meet, Hannah.''

She teased, ''Princess Hannah. It won't do, you know.''

''Nonsense. It has a certain ring. I like it better and better. Queen Hannah the First.''

She laughed at that. The Dowager Duchess of Buccleigh glared back at her from the gilt chair in front of the prince. Hannah smiled and shrugged helplessly, a gesture that further angered the dowager.

Beau had been observing all this low-voiced flirtation with growing impatience. Before the first half of the instrumental concert had ended, he was out of his chair and on his way to the door.

Hannah looked after his retreating back. She remarked innocently to the prince, ''He seems to be cross with me. I wonder why.''

''Not with you, my darling.''

She loved the sound of that but pretended not to hear the endearment for fear she would have to forbid it, like any respectable lady of the *haut ton*.

They started across the hall, with its echo of many chattering voices, and made their way to join the groups in the dining room. Once more, Hannah became aware that Samson Croft was trying to get her attention. He stood against a wall with arms folded. He was alone. He still looked stony-faced, perhaps because his wife had at that minute been approached by Desmond.

The prince saw Hannah's glance in that direction and watched Des carry a glass of champagne to Eulalie Croft. The latter sipped from the glass, then raised one slender little hand to her jaw in a pathetic gesture of pain. The prince frowned.

Hannah asked anxiously, "What are you afraid of? What are you thinking?"

"I wonder. She said it was necessary for Old Samson to be here tonight."

"Why?" She grew more and more unnerved at Prince Andre's tension.

"I wish I knew."

While they watched, Des spoke to Mrs. Croft, indicating the red bruise across her jaw and chin. The princess's hand shook. She stammered something. Des looked furious. His fist clenched. He swung around and stomped across the floor, actually shouldering aside two exquisite young dandies with ambitions to succeed to the dignities of the dethroned Beau Brummel.

Des reached Samson Croft, who looked at him with the grim amusement guaranteed to feed his anger.

"Sir!" Des burst out, loudly enough so that none in the room missed his anger. "You are too old for me to call you out. But by God, no one ever deserved a thrashing more. Your brutality to your exquisite lady is become a byword in Bath." He raised one arm and gave the older man a backhanded slap across the face.

The sound echoed throughout the room and the spacious hall beyond.

Chapter Seventeen

It had all happened in seconds, but Hannah blamed herself. She should have had the foresight to prevent Desmond's demonstration of gallant fury. She tried to make her way through the now noisy gossiping crowd, which had neatly divided pro- and anti-Desmond. But to her astonishment Prince Andre caught her, his strong fingers closing around the pale, bare flesh of her arms just below the shoulders.

"No. Leave this to me. I know the details. None better."

While Prince Andre made his way to the center of the agitated group, where several men, including Colonel Forbin, were trying to draw Des away, Hannah followed the prince, looking for the one person whose stammering and fingering of her "injury" had provoked the shocking scene.

Eulalie Croft was now at the center of the group, huddled behind Samson Croft's solid figure. She seemed to be shivering from the shock of Desmond's appalling public conduct. As for old Samson, he seemed grimly amused by the insulting slap and the humiliation of the scene.

By the time His Highness reached him, Samson was brushing aside expressions of sympathy and regret from those who had taken his part.

"All fustian! Small wonder. I'll not be putting the blame but where's it's best placed."

Prince Andre had reached him and taken his arm. "Let us talk, Sir. Privately."

Desmond Jasper could be heard protesting, "Let me go, damn you! I'm quite aware of what I'm doing. If there's none here that will defend innocence, then it's a task I'll not shirk." His powerful muscles served him well, and he broke free, only to find his sister between him and old Samson.

She had never been more stern, her voice hoarse with anger. "Stop! You are making a cake of yourself over nothing. You and other fools. Come. We are leaving."

"Not I. If Croft wants satisfaction, by God, he shall have it!"

"Des . . ." She got no further. His Highness seemed to have swayed Croft, who waved away the notion of carrying the quarrel onto the dueling field.

"Nay, nay. He was mistook. That's all it be. And here we've gone for to spoil the concert. Go along, *luv*. Where's a lackey? Or that valet of mine? Somebody, call for John Coachman."

Des was still protesting to George Forbin when Hannah heard the prince say to Samson in his quiet voice, "Thank you. You are very wise. Have you known for long?"

Samson rubbed his left thigh with painful grunts.

"Some'ut. I mayn't be wise, but I know a deal about females." He saw Hannah then. Though his wife plucked nervously at his arm, he shrugged off her touch and motioned to Hannah. "Ye've naught to fear, *luv*. Not but what ye've the devil's own spirit. But that great fire-eater is safe at my hands. Run and see to him now."

Hannah touched his hand. "Thank you, Sir. With all my heart."

Des was still complaining that no one need apologize for him, to which he added the rider to Lady Fiona that he didn't in the least understand what this whole affair was about.

Hannah ignored his complaints. Samson Croft limped off with his wife, who continued to give an appearance of fragile helplessness, but Hannah was fascinated by the anguished look the princess gave to Prince Andre as she passed him. Evidently, she had not expected him to betray her trick, which had so nicely fooled the gallant Desmond. As for His Highness, he ignored her pathetic, voiceless plea and looked instead to Hannah.

Hannah had just reached Prince Andre when Beau Croft spoke behind her.

"Shall I take you home? Des is leaving with the colonel."

"Miss Jasper will be quite safe," Prince Andre assured him. "I intend to see her home myself. We have many plans to make."

"Hannah, I believe I have the right to ask you." Beau sounded strained and anxious.

"No." She dismissed him impatiently. "His Highness and I have matters to discuss. Good night, Beau." She felt guilty an instant later, but he had already left her and pushed his way through the slowly dispersing audience.

Ignoring those who remained to see the end of the embarrassing melodrama, Prince Andre put his arm around Hannah's waist, a gesture in itself calculated to arouse gossip.

"You must come to Everdene very soon. Tomorrow? Unless you prefer that the matter be handled by others. But you have always seemed to me the head of your family. And I want you—as my wife."

He must intend to discuss money. Perhaps talk about wedding trips with her income. After his splendid moments in defeating Eulalie Croft's tricks, Hannah found this return to the money-hungry bridegroom a blow to her newfound admiration.

"Tomorrow. The sooner the better. I think I had best go home with Des and George—I mean Colonel Forbin." It hurt to see his puzzled look and to draw her hands out of his firm grasp. He let her go.

"Have I done or said something to offend you? You've changed. In the last minute or so."

"I am sorry." Then she blurted out, "You knew what Mrs. Croft was about, didn't you?"

He hesitated. "She bruises easily. And she knows it."

"By her own hand? Or Samson Croft's hand?"

He looked at her for a long minute. "You know."

She nodded. "And I cannot but admire you for preventing an awkward scene."

His Highness smiled. The smile did not reach his eyes. "You admire me? I might have hoped for more. Do you think you ever will feel more for me?"

"I shouldn't be surprised. That will depend upon you. Tomorrow," she added firmly, knowing that when he heard the news of her supposed income of two thousand pounds his attraction to her would receive a death blow.

He watched her walk away, ignoring the curious stares of her friends. She joined those two powerful guardians of Britain's land and sea, Colonel Forbin and Captain Sir Desmond Jasper. The three of them walked out of the Upper Rooms in a comradely spirit that Andre-Charles-Louis de Bourbon-Valois envied. He had never seen Hannah lovelier, more spirited and exciting. There was challenge in her every move. Her sparkling presence made all else seem pale and flat.

He watched until she was gone from his sight. He was oblivious to the throat-clearings of General Hoogstratten and the rustling of Lady Fiona's new taffeta gown until the general observed, "Unfortunate affair all around. Wretched fellow will scarcely be able to raise his head in the company of anyone who saw him tonight. Shouldn't think the disgrace of it would help that young female, either. That is to say, atop her taste for the grape, so to speak."

"What taste?" the prince asked in a voice the general had not heard since the prince's father found him in bed with a particular bit of muslin that both men had coveted.

General Hoogstratten stammered, "Really, no notion why I said it. Must have heard it repeated and said it without thinking. Regret it most profoundly, Sir."

"You say a deal of things without thinking." He started out of the room and found himself dutifully followed by the general. Without looking back, Prince Andre waved him away. "Take a hired hack and see that Lady Westerby is escorted back with you. I prefer to return alone."

He did not sleep well that night. He was awake early, and, remembering Hannah's democratic notions, deliberately dressed himself before DeVal could choose and arrange his wardrobe for the day. He rode out early with Meiggs to try to view the estate with Hannah's eyes.

"There's a rumor about that you'll be taking a leg shackle, Sir," Meiggs offered.

"Yes. Do you approve?"

"That's for you to say, Highness."

The prince stared. "Very true. But that isn't what you meant, is it?"

"Well, Sir . . ." Meiggs grinned. "Miss Jasper, she mayn't be your sort, or Her Highness's sort, not being royalty-born and all, but she's the kind I'd be putting my blunt on if I was to see her in the ring, or on the track. Clean-limbed, fast in the stretch, and mighty fetching in the victor's circle."

"In short, you prefer Miss Jasper." He saw that Meiggs was watching him intently. He smiled and slapped the groom across the shoulder. "Meiggs, you have excellent taste. And I agree with everything you say. If my efforts at persuasion have ever meant anything, they must serve me now. I am in love with the lady."

"What? You'll be meaning that, Sir? I never thought to see it. What with the princess being so determined and all."

Prince Andre found this highly instructive. "You never liked Her Highness, did you?"

The groom's silence was his answer.

The prince looked around at the summer fields, the grass only just beginning to turn as the first faint scents of autumn crept around them. He said suddenly, only half in jest, "If I might have any gift, I would ask to be Michael Meiggs. Does that amuse you?''

The groom scratched his head. "No, Sir. I'd as lief be Meiggs meself when it comes to that.''

"You would not exchange?''

"With respect, Highness.''

"You are a wise man.''

He had found himself nervous since sunrise, and now, as the morning advanced, he began to wonder if Hannah Jasper lacked enthusiasm for the marriage. Perhaps—God forbid!— he had completely misunderstood her warmth and teasing humor. It might be that she had no interest in him beyond a flirtation. It was hard to know what to think.

He stared around at the green lawns and fields, then back at the house, with its noble palladian front. He had bought it to give Eulalie the kind of frame her portrait needed. Was it Eulalie's house, after all?

He must have looked troubled. Meiggs said abruptly, "If it's the lady that's a worry, I'll lay me best pipe yez'll find it's yourself she loves and not His High and Mighty Highness.''

"This is Eulalie's house," the prince murmured as if he hadn't heard his friend. At Meiggs's surprised question, he waved aside his own words. "No matter, Meiggs. I'll soon know, for good or ill. But," he confessed, "I'd deal rather she loved me than the title.''

"That I'll wager, Sir.''

Although he was still worried and more confused than ever, the prince felt comforted by his friend's shrewd observation.

She did not arrive until after the normal, early dinner hour of the countryside, and Prince Andre had almost given her up. She came with her brother, Des, perched beside him in his phaeton. He handled the reins as he had handled them the night the prince first met Hannah, that is to say, cow-handed, and yet, the sight brought back such warm memories that His Highness wished he might have forever remained "that rascally coachman-groom."

He came down the broad steps to meet the Jaspers, signaling Meiggs to take over the phaeton and its team, which, not surprisingly, appeared spent after almost an hour with Desmond Jasper's hands on the reins.

Des looked bored and dismissed the visit as something his sister had insisted upon. To Prince Andre's relief, he seemed pleased by the appearance on the steps of Lady Fiona Westerby. That lady at once took him off the prince's hands, leaving Hannah to the prince. He thought she looked nervous, a trifle ill-at-ease.

She had been dazzling and exciting last night. Today she was more approachable but no less exciting to his pulses, in a white muslin gown sprigged in a shade of the deepest pink, with a sash to match and a light silk shawl worn loosely over her matching pelisse. Ribbons of the same deep shade tied her hat with its deep poke, and he found himself thinking her lips were very nearly that luscious color. Certainly, they invited him, but he was not at all sure she knew it. She seemed to be singularly unaware of her own physical attractions.

He wondered what her reaction would be if he kissed those soft, tantalizing lips now, with no concern for this shocking display of unbridled passion before the world. But such an act would soon circle the busy little world of Bath and end by proving the gossips' contention that "she was not quite the thing."

Instead, he kissed her fingers and led her into the hall. When he knew that neither Sir Desmond nor Fiona could hear him, and paying little heed to various servants lingering on the ground floor of the house, he tried to let her know his true sentiments.

"You haven't changed your mind, have you, *cherie*? You will accept me?" He went on quickly, "I used to think marriage was possible to me only for dynastic reasons, or for the settlements princes are said to require. But all that is changed now."

"And do not princes still need settlements in their marriages?" she teased him with her lively smile, which seemed to brighten the day.

He was relieved that she had dropped the formality and seriousness that had troubled him during their first few minutes together. He started to remove her shawl with gentle fingers, enjoying the intimacy of her so close to him, but she pulled the shawl back into place with the warning, "I always find it a trifle chilly in these great mansions."

He looked around, beginning to view the austere neo-classic pillars and pilasters and the high, vaulted ceiling with a frown, seeing them in a different light for the first time.

"Come into the little green salon. It is much more intimate, and Abercrombie will have the tea tray brought." He looked into her face, trying to banish his own tension with a mischievous suggestion that was only half in jest. "I want very much to kiss you. In fact, I will."

She flushed a little and almost seemed to withdraw as he tilted her chin up and sealed her surprised mouth with his own. The touch and taste of her stimulated him to bring up the matter of their marriage and their future. He was enjoying himself so thoroughly with this kiss that it was only when she began to struggle that he realized he had left her, and himself, breathless.

"I'll not apologize. Don't expect it," he warned her.

She laughed, but she did not seem to share his delight in their brief moment of passion. It disappointed him and worried him too. He took a breath and braced himself.

"Hannah, do you mean to refuse me?"

"Not I. No. And yet, and yet . . ."

"Then come. Tell me what changes you will make here in your house."

She looked around, toward the north view from the long windows and doors looking out upon the kitchen garden, the stables and fields. She walked away from him, touching the furniture, the sofa table in the middle of the long room, then a torchère near one of the doors opening out upon the north terrace. She stood staring out through the glass door until he could no longer refrain from asking, "What concerns you, my love?" She stiffened at the unconscious endearment, which made him smile. He joined her in three or four slow strides, taking her resistant form in his arms, wondering how to restore to her that ripple of laughter and the sparkle that made him know she enjoyed his company as much as he enjoyed hers.

"Can you be happy here?" he asked, trying to refrain from showing how troubled he was by her curious mood. It began to be borne upon him that she might not love him, or his style of life, or the formality, though this was far less formal than his father's style.

Hannah shook her head. "It must cost a great deal to support an estate. I shouldn't think it would be profitable."

It was the last thing in the world he had expected. He knew few women of Miss Jasper's class and none whatever in Eulalie's world who knew or cared a jot about the profitability of a great estate.

He agreed casually, because he knew hardly more than Eulalie would have known.

"Probably not."

She looked at him with something like indignation, an emotion whose source baffled him.

"And you don't care?"

He was bewildered, but since she seemed to set such store by commercial knowledge, he tried to please her.

"Only when I cannot pay my way in life. I don't propose to live upon my retinue and followers, as my—as others may have done." He smiled winningly, reminding her, "Your friend Meiggs the groom would doubtless pay his way in life, but he was lucky. He need not live like a prince."

Now he was concerned by her frown and the steady, unsmiling look in her hazel eyes as she said, "I am persuaded that you must have quite different notions. But they will not do. You cannot support the extravagances of this estate on an income of two thousand pounds per annum."

He laughed. "Certainly not." The laughter faded quickly. "Why two thousand?"

She took a breath, licked her delectable lips, and blurted out, "Because that is my income per year."

The words lingered on the cooling air of late afternoon.

She added nervously, "Most of my fortune is in keeping for my children and their children."

He remembered long afterward that his fingers gripped her slim waist, and how his first thought had been, She imagined she was marrying a wealthy scion of royalty. I will lose her. The pressure must have hurt her, but she gave no sign of it. Even her possible pain did not disturb him in this moment. He was too concerned with himself; he could not let her go. She was so exactly the woman to make him happy. But evidently, he could not make her happy. She would never marry a poor man, a man whose credit was all in his ancient past. Or would she?

With the touch of her, and her closeness, he gathered courage to ask the most important question, a question that would never have occurred to his ancestors:

"Do you love me?"

Her smile flickered and faded, but he read the answer in her face and felt an enormous relief.

"You know that I do."

"And of course I love you. So much for basic matters." Hoping to relieve the tension between them in the way they had both found to be a delight, he remarked gravely, "But I daresay you are right. I must marry where I shall be properly housed and supported." He sighed. "Now, let us consider. Have you a candidate?"

With an unaccustomed lack of expression she volunteered, "There is Clarissa Tremoyle. I am told her settlement upon a suitable bridegroom will be a very warm one."

He pretended to think this over, only to dismiss the girl with a fine show of reluctance.

"A pity she has black hair. She would have done very

well. But, quite impossible. My children must have chestnut hair. It is a family tradition."

This time she had developed a little gleam of a smile. "Dare I point out that your own hair is very nearly black?"

"And look at the pass I have come to. No. She will not do."

"Perhaps you should look abroad. There is Marie Antoinette's daughter. She is very high in royal counsels, now that her uncle has been propped upon the French throne."

"Quite ineligible. She belongs to d'Angouleme, I believe. And besides, I could never marry a Hapsburg. Those appalling noses."

"From all I have observed in their portraits, there is little to choose between Hapsburg and Bourbon noses."

"Oh, but you will allow, my own nose is unexceptionable."

She looked up, touched the bridge of his nose, and agreed demurely, "Very handsome, I'm sure." But her eyes failed to mirror the laughter on her lips as she added, "Well, then, what shall we do? I cannot conceive of Your Highness living upon two thousand a year."

All manner of ideas had been whirling through his brain, and he reminded her suddenly, "But Michael Meiggs could do so, very comfortably."

"You are not Michael Meiggs."

"I was. Once. And happy to be so." Ideas paraded past his vision. He took her hands and led her to the central doors. "What do you see?"

"The kitchen gardens—you mean to be a gardener?"

"To your right, where Meiggs has just come out, this side of the cow-shed. My stables."

She rested her head back briefly against his cheek.

"You are a prince of a royal house. You can never be a groom."

"But I can breed horses," he pointed out in triumph. "I offered seven thousand pounds to hold Everdene Hall. I shall put it on the block. It will easily sell. Then I will invest a portion of the seven thousand in more breeding stock and a neat little property. The rest we may invest in the funds or whatever else we choose." He looked into her eyes. "Could you be content as the wife of a horse breeder?"

She burst into the merry, delicious laugh he had longed to hear.

"I do believe you mean it."

"Certainly I do." He began to make plans, aware that for the first time in his life there was no weight of centuries upon his shoulders. He was free, after twenty-nine years. "I have only to assure myself that those who have been loyal to me are well cared for. Abercrombie. Yes. I know just the household for him. A Bavarian duke with a taste for beautiful . . . but enough of that. Meiggs would come with me. And DeVal. Ah, but poor Fiona!"

Hannah asked unexpectedly, "Was she ever your mistress?"

"Good Lord, no! She belonged to my father. That is to say, they were great friends. She has been like a mother to me."

"Not a mother."

"A sister? Poor Fiona."

Hannah seemed to be more amused by his earnest and exciting plans than she should have been.

"Poor Fiona, you called her. How extremely fortunate!"

"I don't see how."

"Because," she explained, "my brother is a knight-errant. He dotes upon rescuing beautiful ladies who are in difficulties."

Remembering the unfortunate result of Eulalie's tricks, he murmured, "So I noticed," but he smiled at her simple solution. "You and I are to play matchmakers, I collect."

"We will mention her problem several times, and with a trifling help from Lady Fiona it should serve very well."

Overcome by the entire fairy tale atmosphere of his prospective new life, he kissed her hair just above the warm, smooth column of her neck.

"How glad I am that you are not a great heiress! It would have been so prosaic."

She was unexpectedly sobered by this remark. "Will you be sorry to lose Everdene?"

He waved it away. "Relieved. I made the purchase to house Her Highness, and I seem to find myself a stranger in it. Save for the stables, of course."

She was amused by that and would have returned his kiss, but her hand closed on his suddenly as she looked behind him. He heard footsteps and the sweep of Lady Fiona's gown and turned, wondering at the surprise on Hannah's face.

He felt more than surprise at sight of Beaufort Croft dressed for riding, looking breathless and blown-about. He had come in hurriedly between Fiona and Sir Desmond, simply bursting with news.

"Hannah, you are needed."

Prince Andre looked at Fiona, who shrugged and raised her eyebrows. He could not resist the observation, "What, Mr. Croft? Are we to have the pleasure of your company still again? What can be Everdene's lure, I wonder?"

Beau Croft's faintly slanting eyes regarded him with very little liking.

"As a matter of fact, I cannot stay to discuss the matter, Your Highness. I have been sent to conduct Hannah—Miss Jasper, to my grandfather. It is Old Samson's order."

The prince glanced at Hannah, who looked more cross than he had ever seen her.

"Beau, have you taken leave of your senses? How can you march into a house where you were uninvited and make such an absurd demand? Mr. Croft doesn't order me about. You came here solely to cause difficulties between . . ." She broke off in confusion, aware that the prince enjoyed her tirade prodigiously. ". . . At all events, I know why you came."

Sir Desmond was completely baffled. He complained to Lady Fiona, ''Old Croft was once Hannah's friend in her childhood. But there can be no reason, no excuse, for this intrusion upon her life. Why would he wish to see Hannah now?''

''Perhaps to explain or make his apologies for last night, I should imagine.''

Hannah said, ''That is nonsense. He has nothing to apologize for. He behaved with impeccable manners.''

''What? Now, see here, Hannah!''

Before brother and sister could get into a brangle over the matter, Prince Andre reminded Hannah, ''Darling, perhaps I should go instead. I think when Croft discovers our plans, he will be the first to congratulate us.''

''No!'' Everyone stared at Beau. He added firmly, ''I did not wish to disturb you, but the truth of the matter is, my grandfather became ill in the night. The matter at the Upper Rooms overset him, and he took syrup of poppies in order to sleep. He suffers from several ailments. A rheumatic problem. And the gout. I think the overdose of the sleeping syrup frightened him. Perhaps he wishes to speak about his will. Something of that sort. He was most insistent. Only Hannah.''

''I should not be surprised,'' Sir Desmond put in. ''The old ogre always had a fondness for Hannah.''

The prince did not like this quick end to a wonderful hour with his love. He liked even less the notion of sending her off in Beau Croft's company.

''I'll go with you. We can tell him our news together. I think it will please him.''

''He will see no one,'' Beau insisted. ''Not even me. Mrs. Croft said he refuses to discuss the matter with her. It must be Hannah. Alone.''

Hannah said, ''I think I understand. He confided in me one day in the Pump Room. I will go, of course.''

''And I will go,'' the prince added. ''I will wait for Miss Jasper.''

Beau Croft reminded him, "My grandfather has taken a violent dislike to you, Sir. If you choose to visit the Crofts, I suggest we keep your presence a secret from the old gentleman. At his age, there is always a danger that the slightest shock may carry him off."

"He is right, my dearest," Hannah told him.

Beau Croft seemed to pale at her endearment, but since these were the first words of love she had ever used to the prince, they affected His Highness so strongly he framed her face between his hands and kissed her before them all. When he let her go he promised, "As you wish, *cherie*. We will continue to make our plans for the horse-breeding farm sooner than you imagine."

This puzzled both Lady Fiona and Sir Desmond, but it only increased Beau Croft's disturbance. He said abruptly, "I return to my grandfather's lodgings. Des, will you be good enough to carry Hannah to the Crescent?"

"If I am unwelcome," the prince reminded him, "I should imagine Sir Desmond would be even less welcome."

Des exploded, "Well, damn! I'll set Hannah down at the Royal Crescent and not return until Hannah sends for me."

Beau was impatient to be gone. "Samson Croft's man will take Hannah home."

It was not what the prince would have wished, but it mattered very little. He planned to visit the Jasper House in Queen Square by the time darkness fell. She would have returned home by then. He lingered over her hand, looking into her eyes and reading there a love he could not doubt.

Then she left with her brother. Beau hurried past them and out to his curricle. Prince Andre turned to Fiona.

"Congratulate me. I am to become the proud owner of a splendid little horse-breeding farm, with which I shall support my enchanting bride."

He found it understandable that she stared. She had probably never believed him capable of supporting himself, much less a wife. He had never been more proud to confound the world.

Chapter Eighteen

"I can't think what was in the old ogre's mind," Des complained while Hannah sat up straighter, bracing herself for the meeting with Samson Croft and his princess-wife.

"I daresay, at eighty-six, he thinks of settling his affairs. It is quite possible he doesn't trust either his wife or his grandson. At all events, I had that impression when I talked to him in the Pump Room."

Des shook his head. "It would be most improper if he left his fortune away from his wife, after all she has endured. And he certainly cannot think it proper to leave it with you."

Hannah grimaced. "I devoutly hope not. I've only just settled to make a happy marriage on two thousand a year and the profits of horse-breeding. It would be too much to expect me to explain away another fortune besides my own."

"What!"

"Nothing. Samson Croft is asking to see me . . ."

"Demanding."

"Just so. But only to ask my advice. I shouldn't be the least surprised if he wishes to know my view of your unconscionable conduct at the Upper Rooms last night. I shall tell him."

Contrary to her expectations, he did not attempt to argue with her on the matter of Eulalie Croft's ill treatment. Was it possible he had begun to share her suspicions? If so, he was not the only man who believed young Mrs. Croft had some-how acquired her bruises through her own contrivance. She now knew Prince Andre thought so.

Prince Andre. Who loved her for herself and not for her fortune. He was willing to sacrifice rank and princely proto-col for love of her. She had never believed it possible. She hugged her arms, imagining his own embrace warmed her now in the growing dusk. She knew quite well that any of a dozen heiresses would be only too happy to become his wife, Princess de Bourbon-Valois. She still couldn't imag-ine what a man, a prince, who looked like Andre-Charles, could find in plain Hannah Jasper that would make him sac-rifice so much.

Desmond said, obviously as the result of deep reflection or the result of very recent persuasion, "I'm told that Her Highness—I mean Mrs. Croft—bruises easily. There are those that have even seen her bruise herself. If she turns sud-denly and runs upon a sideboard or a table."

"I shouldn't be at all surprised."

"I mean to say, the old man may, by accident, have—"
She looked at him. He subsided.

"Well, you'll find the straight of it, I make no doubt. What are your plans with His Highness? Can he be such a sapskull he believes you are poor?"

She put a hand on his wrist anxiously. "Please say noth-ing. It will only ruin our plans. He is genuinely happy to be a horse-breeder."

"Good God! What will you do when he discovers the truth?"

"He won't. I shall make over most of my holdings in a trust for our children, perhaps with a portion to come to me when I am twenty-five. Some such flummery."

Des surrendered the argument with the admission, "I've always found money to be damned useful. Frankly, I shouldn't like to find myself without a feather to fly with. Mighty good to know there's a deal more of the blunt where that came from."

"Luckily, I'm not marrying you."

He grinned. "Lucky for me. You're a mighty managing female."

She considered his words and agreed. "But I don't mean to be so with His Highness. In his quiet way he wouldn't permit it."

She saw the pale Bath stone of the Royal Crescent loom up in the gathering darkness and girded herself for the meeting to come. Like her brother, she still wondered what, precisely, Samson Croft wanted to discuss with her. It would be an embarrassing event, no matter what the subject might be. It was certain to involve either his wife or his grandson. Perhaps both.

Beau Croft was waiting for them inside the wrought-iron fencing in front of the steps. He was still highly nervous. It seemed obvious that he expected the worst from her visit to his grandfather. Taking her arm, he promised Desmond, "I'll have her home properly in a closed carriage, but the old—my grandfather is asleep now, so it may be some while before Hannah can see him."

Des scowled. "Shall I take you home, Hannah? No point in your standing about waiting to be called in. You aren't some kitchenmaid on your preferment."

She smiled up at him and waved him away. "No, dear, thank you. But I shall manage. You said I am a very managing woman." She added, while she felt Beau Croft's muscles tighten under her hand, "And I have so much to think about. So much happiness."

"As you wish."

Hannah and Beau went up the inside staircase together. Hannah noticed the artistic signs of the Princess Eulalie everywhere, from the delicate miniatures and silhouettes to the exquisite bowl of yellow roses on the credenza at the head of the stairs. She was wondering if her own taste would disappoint the prince but consoled herself with the thought that he must see their difference by now.

She became aware again of Beau's tension. Before she

could question him, he asked abruptly, "Do you mean to marry that princeling?"

"I mean to marry a horse-breeder named Andre-Charles."

He scorned the pretense. "You must be aware that he was hanging out for an heiress."

"At one time. Like you."

"Don't be flippant, for God's sake! The difference is, I've always loved you."

In his circumstances, and remembering the many times he had taken advantage of the "heiress," she could only laugh. This seemed to bring out all the dark aspects of his nature. He said coldly, "If you will be good enough to wait in Eulalie's study. It is a trifle cool this evening. There is a fire, and you will find ladies' magazines. *La Belle Assemblée*, *La Mode de Paris*, that sort of thing."

"And Mrs. Croft? Is she with her husband?"

"No." He bit that off. One of the Croft parlor-maids opened the door of Mrs. Croft's study and curtsied as Hannah went in. Beau called to Hannah, "He won't see her. God knows what's in his mind, but if we can persuade him that she genuinely cares for his welfare, he may speak to you in quite a different vein."

The stout little parlor-maid bobbed another curtsy and hurried away. Beau would have followed, but Hannah called to him.

"Beau, wait. Tell me something."

He hesitated but came in to join her, standing over her where she sat on the edge of the loveseat before the low-burning hearth fire. "What do you want to know?"

"What happened to Samson Croft last night?"

He grasped the sharp corner of the mantel. She had clearly shocked him.

"Happened? What the devil do you mean?" He saw that his violent reaction had surprised her and recovered rather shakily. "I beg pardon. I didn't understand. I thought—I hardly know what I thought. You see, Grandfather takes his medicines as he chooses. No one has ever given him orders, even about the pain he suffers. And he does suffer."

"I know."

He slapped the mantel. "He will not listen. I'm convinced he must have taken the damned syrup twice. He was asleep, and Eulalie could not wake him. We called in the apothecary and the old man's surgeon. Eventually, he came to himself. He was furious, of course. He called for Madeira. Why Madeira, I shall never know. But he refused to see us afterward."

"Where is his wife?"

He raised his head. "Sitting outside his door. Waiting. She is very devoted to him. And of course, she feels responsible for that awkward business with your brother."

"I am not surprised."

"Because she realizes that she bruises so easily. Old Samson probably doesn't mean to mistreat her. He touches her a bit roughly, and the damage is done."

"Oh, fustian!"

He opened his eyes at that and started to say something but bit it off, looking angry again.

"How long must I wait?" she demanded.

He tugged hard at the worn bellpull, and in less than five minutes another maid arrived with a tea tray, expansive with cakes and toast and jellies, everything to occupy her mind and body while she awaited the call of Samson Croft in curiosity and some uneasiness.

Seeing that she was growing more impatient, Beau went away to discover if his grandfather was ready for her yet. She was encouraged when Eulalie Croft came by and looked in. The princess was beautiful as ever, in a visiting gown of a deep blue silk and a paisley shawl, but her features seemed to be strained and she certainly looked her age. She was upward of twenty-six. She must care a little for her husband. Her tension and manner revealed this, and for Samson Croft's sake, Hannah hoped so, but knowing the world somewhat, Hannah thought it more likely that her apprehension was rooted in a fear that he would make new provisions in his will.

When Hannah had finished a cup of very bitter tea and nibbled at a northcountry scone dripping with butter, Eulalie observed plaintively, "He has dozed off again. It is provoking when he made such a to-do about seeing you."

"Doubtless he will be in better frame to see me tomorrow."

Hannah began to gather up her reticule and prepare to leave.

But Eulalie insisted nervously, "Oh, please. If we could settle it tonight, it would be a great relief. Just give him half an hour more. Or a few minutes. One more cup of tea. I will join you."

Reluctantly, Hannah yielded. She, too, wanted to settle Samson Croft's problem so that she might be free to make plans about her future with Prince Andre.

Eulalie stood by the little drop-leaf table where the tea set had been placed and poured brandy from a decanter into a French crystal glass. As she was about to drink, she recollected her guest and poured a similar amount for her while describing Samson's accidental overdose. Her story was so like Beau's that Hannah wondered if she and her "grandson" had rehearsed it.

While Hannah absently sipped the brandy she watched Eulalie and asked questions several times. It seemed likely that she had checked her story against Beau's, but there could scarcely be anything criminal in that. The reason for it, however, would be intriguing.

Meanwhile, the waiting made Hannah sleepy and she yawned, begging pardon.

"I'm afraid this business of waiting has made me bad company. If Mr. Croft will not see me now, I really must go."

Eulalie breathed deeply and went away to make certain that her husband knew Miss Jasper was waiting.

By the time she returned Hannah had finished the few

swallows of brandy and was ready to leave. The heat of the fire and the stuffiness of the room gave her a headache, and even the thought of descending the long white staircase to the street floor appeared to be an ordeal. She wished very much that she hadn't come. It had been an absurd business. As though Mr. Croft couldn't afford solicitors to manage his affairs! He certainly had no need of a casual acquaintance like Hannah Jasper.

Nevertheless, Eulalie was excessively grateful to her, following her to the hall and the staircase, ordering the plump maid to deliver her down to Beau Croft.

"Oh, and Miss Jasper," she called as Hannah carefully made her way down the stairs, "I have received a hint that you and His Highness may make a match of it. May I offer my good wishes to you? A splendid triumph."

"Triumph?" Hannah echoed, stopping on the stairs and holding tight to the handrail while she grimaced at her own extraordinary tiredness.

"This is to say, His Highness could never marry anyone about whom there was a breath of scandal. But then, clearly, you qualify."

"I certainly hope so."

At the bottom of the stairs, Beau came forward to give her his hand. It must have grown suddenly cold outside. He was wearing a many-caped coachman's greatcoat and tricorne hat and apologized for Hannah's summer frock, her light pelisse and shawl.

"But I have Samson's big chaise ready. Being closed, it should be warmer, and the journey isn't far."

"Don't be nonsensical. I walk far greater distances by daylight. Do let us be gone. I have a headache. I think I need my dinner."

"Here. Good Lord, Hannah! Do hold tight to my arm. You nearly trod on the butler's cat. Are you quite the thing?"

"Quite. I had a little brandy. A very little. But it made me sleepy."

"Oh. I daresay that explains it."

Scudding clouds cut off the moon and the night was unexpectedly black. Autumn had made its presence known. She let herself be helped into the heavy, closed carriage and settled back, huddling against the clammy atmosphere of the interior.

She wondered vaguely why Beau did not join her and then realized that, for some reason, he must be up on the coachman's box. She let her head fall back against the worn cushions and closed her eyes, wondering where Prince Andre was at this moment and what he was about.

The four-horse team started off at its own deliberate pace but soon found itself beyond the gleaming Crescent and moving down one of Bath's familiar hills toward Queen Square.

Her thoughts blurred into a semi-sleep that was disturbed when the coach swayed and jerked suddenly as the horses were given the signal to turn left.

She tried to sit up but found it an effort. They must have turned into Queen Square from the west end. She would soon be home, thank heaven! She tried again, reached the window and looked out, then blinked in confusion. They had passed the railings of Queen Square on her right, which meant that they were turning toward Milsom Street.

She started to rap on the window, but her knuckles seemed turned to water. She was still fighting to regain strength and to scream when her sight blurred again and despite all her efforts, she sank back weakly, fighting to remain conscious.

Chapter Nineteen

Miss Quilling was not easily impressed. She had been known to remark firmly, "I am an English gentlewoman, and Queen Charlotte herself can boast of no more."

"Rather less," Hannah had answered with a smile. "She is not English."

But even Miss Quilling was a trifle flustered when His Royal Highness came to Queen Square that evening, "on an errand of supreme importance to me," as he confided.

She stammered a welcome and would have ushered him into the little salon where Hannah's beaux regularly collected to wait for her, but he stopped her. His brown eyes were alight and he seemed almost as nervous as Miss Quilling found herself.

During the two hours that had passed since he said goodbye to Hannah he had broken the news of his coming marriage to his own household and found them badly divided. Meiggs was not in the least surprised. His only remark was that "yez'll excuse the liberty, Sir, but I'd have thought it was settled soon as you played meself in them games of groom and all."

Lady Fiona Westerby was delighted, and the prince felt secure enough to promise her, "Yours may well be the next Jasper wedding."

It was a different matter with Abercrombie and DeVal. His father's ex-procurer obviously felt that he should marry no less than a current royal heiress, that his title and lineage should be bartered to the highest bidder and be damned to happiness.

As to DeVal, he was even more insulting, even going so far as to hint at the gossip about Miss Jasper and her supposed fondness for spirits.

"Where did you hear these lies?" the prince demanded.

DeVal had looked despairing. It was only after the prince's stern insistence amounting to a command that he confessed, "The general mentioned it, but I found it difficult to believe, until . . ."

"Yes?"

"Her Highness, the Princess Eulalie knew about the lady on the Abbey steps. She said there could be no doubt. Several persons identified a cloak and bonnet worn by the person who staggered about the Abbey yard and once fell upon the steps. Very similar to ones worn by Miss Jasper. And knowing her reputation, well—what else could they think? Your Highness knows how tongues wag."

"I do, indeed." The prince was aware of a grim certainty that he had never quite admitted. He knew the day Eulalie visited Everdene that she was responsible for the suspicions of brutality circulated against her husband. Now, with DeVal's remarks, he suspected Eulalie's complicity again. Whether she had somehow managed to plant the seed of the lies about Hannah or simply profited by that idiot Hoogstratten's babble, he could not be sure. Nor did he know how someone who looked like Hannah had been seen on the Abbey steps. But Lalie was involved in the matter.

He said, "How far have you spread Mrs. Croft's lie?"

DeVal was alarmed. "Her Highness merely trusted you would consider the other young heiresses because you owed it to your name not to taint it with something of that sort."

"When was this? When the princess visited Everdene?"

Caught by surprise, DeVal thought back to the moment he had first heard the story from Eulalie Croft. He was pleased to say with a certain pride, "No, sir. Long ago. On the day of the waltzing party. She rode by and you were out visiting your farm coteens, as Meiggs calls them.''

All that he said after the words ''waltzing party'' was lost on His Highness. He startled and unnerved the valet by the hard triumph in his face and manner.

''She told you about finding Miss Jasper on the Abbey Steps? My dear DeVal, the event had not occurred at that time. As a matter of truth, it was arranged to occur sometime after Mrs. Croft left for Yorkshire, the following morning.''

He had not waited for DeVal's reaction. He was not sure what he would do about the valet, but he left him abruptly and ordered Meiggs to bring around Zephine, his favorite mount.

He decided that Hannah should know in the very first moment possible that the lies about her had been traced to their source. He wanted to swear to her as well that Eulalie Croft must counter these lies with the truth. ''It had been a malicious piece of rumor.'' Otherwise, he would cause the entire truth to be known by every citizen of Bath.

Perhaps Hannah would want the entire truth known in any case. She deserved to make the decision.

Miss Quilling had apparently been told about the marriage, because she greeted the prince with considerable pleasure, though none of the fawning that he had discovered was often false. He must start to break down his own reserve. Tonight he would become a ''horse-breeder named Andre de Bourbon-Valois.'' The name was still too long, too absurdly royal. He searched through a score of family names, hesitated over several lesser families who had won their way in by marriage, and decided to leave the choice with Hannah.

''Miss Quilling, congratulate me. Your enchanting charge has done me the honor of accepting my proposal. May I see her now? And then her good brother?''

The lady contained her enthusiasm, but her eyes were happy, and when he offered his hand in the middle of her curtsy, she hesitated, then accepted his hand a trifle uneasily.

"Sir Desmond is in the billiard rooms, but I regret to say, Miss Jasper hasn't returned home yet."

The news might not have been disturbing twenty-four hours earlier. Even today, before his talk with DeVal, the question of her safety would not occur to him. Now the idea haunted him. His grip on her hand tightened until she mumbled, "If you please, sir," and he let her go in embarrassment. But she was not fooled.

"You are troubled, Your Highness? I confess, I should feel more comfortable if she were elsewhere than with the Crofts. But of course, Sir Desmond is not concerned."

"He hasn't my knowledge of our friend Mrs. Croft."

"But I don't understand. Surely, Her Highness will see that Miss Hannah is safe. I mean, if Old Samson becomes violent."

He didn't stay to explain. He had already turned away to find Desmond while Miss Quilling looked out between the heavy gold-fringed drapes, protesting anxiously, "Mr. Beaufort Croft is there. I have little regard for him, but he and Hannah have been friends since time out of mind." She cheered up a minute later. "There! You see? Coming down the Gay Street hill. Mr. Samson Croft's carriage. It will turn in at the Square and all our little fears are done."

Prince Andre stopped in the doorway. "Has it turned?"

She stood rigid and watchful. Then she grasped a handful of the gold fringe on the portiere. "How extraordinary! For an instant I thought I made out Hannah's face at the window in the glow of the carriage lights. But no. The team is turning toward the town. Surely, not at this hour. It must be deserted, even for the Abbey. Except, naturally, for the hotels in Stall Street."

Prince Andre knew in this moment that all his fears had not been groundless.

"Are you certain the coach belonged to Croft?"

Her voice trembled slightly. "I have known Mr. Samson

Croft for forty years. I do know that wretched coach. He has used it for the past score of years."

He wondered if Eulalie and her fellow conspirator, probably Beaufort Croft, had decided to stage another performance in the Abbey yard. He felt suddenly chilled. If this was their plan, to disgrace Hannah, it might explain why they had enticed her to the Croft lodgings.

He looked out in the hall. There was no time to lose. "Captain! Captain, where the devil are you?"

Desmond Jasper loped out into the entry hall on the ground floor to demand, "What's afoot? Who's bellowing for me like a bo'sun's mate?"

Mrs. Plackett appeared from her own parlor near the kitchen to demand, "What has happened? Is anything amiss?"

Both men ignored her. The prince rushed down the stairs two at a time.

"Take up a cloak of some kind, Captain. We've no time to lose. Your sister may be in danger. I'm on my way now."

"What? Danger?" All the same, the fellow reacted with naval promptness. In a minute Mrs. Plackett had given him an old storm cape, which he dragged around his shoulders while he trooped after the prince, out of the house and into Queen Square.

He caught up with the prince as they crossed deserted Gay Street under the flickering street lights. The prince explained to him briefly.

Jasper found it hard to believe Eulalie's part in all this. "Though I've never liked Beau above half. He's back of it, I'll lay you odds."

The prince shrugged. "He may be, but Lalie is in this up to her pretty neck, and by God, if they have hurt Hannah in any way—!"

Sir Desmond held out his knotted fists. "If you are in the right of it, I'll strangle them—Beau, at all events—with my bare hands."

"Young Croft said old Samson had taken an overdose of

a drug. A form of opium, I should think. If Croft has murdered the old man, the hangman will save you the trouble.''

They saw no one at this hour on usually busy Milsom Street and turned down toward the Abbey, the Pump Room, and the White Hart Inn and Tavern. By this time they were on the run, Sir Desmond panting a little. Two carriages and a hackney coach waited outside the hotel, and an elderly drunk wove his way toward the Avon River some distance past the ancient stone site of the Abbey.

In the yard between the Abbey and the darkened Pump Room, the heavy Croft coach and four restive horses waited. A lean young man in coachman's greatcoat and tricorne hat had laid a bundled figure upon the Abbey step and was feeling in his pockets for something.

Prince Andre's raised hand warned his companion and they approached silently across the cobblestones.

In his exertions Beau Croft's tricorne hat had fallen off and he was clearly recognizable, but he was too busy to rescue it.

Doubtless he considered himself safe. No other pedestrian was on the streets at the moment. He had located a bottle that appeared to be spirits of some kind, and with the same hand raised Hannah's head and shoulders against the crook of his arm. She looked very pale, but the prince saw her move slightly, though her eyes remained closed.

Thank God, she was alive!

Beau uncorked the bottle, setting the cork on the cobblestone beside him. At that instant Prince Andre's highly polished Hessian boot came down hard upon his outspread fingers. He screamed with pain, trying to free his hand and at the same time strain to see over his shoulder. He had little time to move further. The captain's muscular arm went around his throat, like a heavy serpent, closing in and holding him securely in a stranglehold.

He would have dropped the bottle, but the prince set it aside on the step and took Hannah into his arms. Lovingly, he brushed the tangled hair out of her eyes, coaxing her in a low voice, "Come, sweetheart, wake up. You are safe now. We'll soon have you home . . . Wake up. *Cherie*, can you hear me?" He looked up. "Damn him! He's drugged her."

"No!" Beau choked, his eyes almost starting from his head at the unbearable pressure from Desmond Jasper's arm. "Only a little. To make drowsy. Love her . . . I wouldn't . . ." He tried again, hoarsely. ". . . Wouldn't hurt her."

"You would merely make it appear that she was drunk."

"Wouldn't do that. That witch . . . her notion. No part of inheritance if I refused."

"Let me break his neck," Sir Desmond begged.

"Her eyes are open. Can you hear me, my darling? Look at me. Feeling more the thing?"

Hannah tried to smile. "Nothing, truly. Only a headache. Some drug, I think. In the tea."

Sir Desmond's muscles tightened and Beau made a gasping, gurbling sound. Hannah raised one hand weakly.

"Don't, please. Just send him away. Oh, thank God, you came." She blinked. "And Des, too? Don't strangle him, for heaven's sake!"

"He deserves it," the prince remarked. "But I suppose it would be a trifle awkward. People are bound to ask why."

Hannah shook her head and then groaned at the effort. "Do something else. To make him go away."

The prince adjusted her position and in doing so, felt the bottle of brandy and an idea came to him.

"He was going to make her drink this."

"Not drink," Beau protested. "Just pour over her."

The prince nodded. "Of course. But what a waste! I have a better idea. If you please, Mr. Croft, drink."

"No!" He began to struggle. "Throat sore. Couldn't."

"Drink!"

Desmond Jasper released his pressure ever so little and Beau made the effort. It must have been painful, but he managed a few swallows.

"Go on."

"Impossible."

"Go on!"

Beau drank while Hannah and her rescuers watched. He made further, desperate protests, but they fell upon unyielding stone, as did he himself some little time later.

"What shall we do now? Leave him here?" Sir Desmond asked as the Prince carefully placed the empty bottle in Beau's slack fingers.

"Not quite yet. Hannah, my love, give me your bonnet."

The hat hung from the back of her neck by its luscious dark pink ribbons. Not quite understanding, she let him untie it, then while she gaped in astonishment, he set it on the back of Beau's head, where the world could see Beau's own good-looking face and hair.

"That should do it. To anyone who sees him, it is clear he has been masquerading as Miss Jasper."

"We used to masquerade as children," Hannah remembered suddenly. "At a distance we were almost of one size." She groaned again. "I have a dreadful headache."

The prince was firm. "We must get you home at once. In Samson Croft's carriage."

It seemed an appropriate repayment after the rough ride Hannah had received from the Crescent to the Abbey.

Prince Andre insisted on carrying her to the coach, although she assured him she could walk. Despite her firm objections, he bundled her up and dropped her among the cushions of the old coach, then got in beside her. She giggled a little hysterically at the thought of her brother acting as coachman, and the prince was so relieved at her recovery that he was able to join in her amusement.

Sir Desmond got them home safely but at once gave over the team and coach to Jemie for the return to the Croft stables. The prince wanted to sit with Hannah while she recovered, but here Miss Quilling was firm. She did, however, look the other way when the prince insisted on kissing Hannah good night.

Hannah ever afterward claimed that it was this kiss, bestowed on her lips with his unique combination of tenderness and passion, rather than Miss Quilling's remedies that cured her of her headache.

He was back in Queen Square again shortly after sunup, but by this time Hannah was well into a good night's sleep, and Miss Quilling refused to wake her until almost noon.

It was while she was dressing and, according to Miss Quilling, "speaking with some warmth about Your Highness," that the Jaspers had an unexpected caller. Sir Desmond came up the stairs to announce to Prince Andre in unbelieving tones,

"It's the old ogre himself. Limping out of that huge coffin of a carriage we returned last night."

The prince felt something very like relief. "Sooner or later, Croft must face his wife's treachery. I had intended to visit him as soon as I assure myself about Hannah."

"Well, damn, let him come. But if his wife is involved, we may as well know it. And if he doesn't make her suffer, I shall, by Gad!"

"Ye may take it that the lady is proper paid, gentlemen."

Both men turned abruptly. Samson Croft stood in the doorway, leaning on his cane with both palms pressed hard on the ivory head. His face looked much as it always did, heavy and stern, the thick lips highly colored, but his deep-set eyes glistened under the shaggy gray brows. It was hard to know whether that gleam was amusement or hatred. Perhaps a little of both.

Prince Andre recovered his voice first.

"Then you are aware of Mrs. Croft's part in the maligning of Miss Jasper?"

"If 'e mean to say the business about my grandson that was found bosky—no, sodden drunk—on the Abbey steps, I've me own ideas about that. I make no doubt it's long deserved. He was found by the Duchess of Buccleigh on her way to church, and vastly shocked she was."

The captain and Prince Andre grinned at each other, but Samson Croft went on. "As to me bride, the faithful lass that did me the honor to marry old Samson, she's had a mite of bad luck.''

"Bad luck?" the prince asked. "How?"

The old man ignored this. He turned to Sir Desmond.

"Well now. What else? She tried to have me killed by you, young Jasper. A duel that failed, eh? So she tries to get old Samson to take overdoses of that damned poppy drug. But I'm too spry for that. I watched her try to dose my wine, and I caught her last night.''

Sir Desmond cried, "Good God! But will she try again?"

"Not likely. She wanted my fortune, of course. But now, she's agreed to a divorce. I have the lass's confession. It's a hanging offense. But I've a kind heart. I just saw her off on a sea voyage to the Antipodes, her and my bosky grandson. They'll not come back, for fear of prison or the rope.''

Sir Desmond burst into laughter, and even the prince thought it better than Eulalie deserved, in the circumstances. He had felt responsible for Lalie's tricks, believing conceitedly that she might have played off her crimes out of love for him, but he knew now that a fortune had always been Eulalie's goal since she first made her decision to marry the aged man.

Sir Desmond remarked wryly to the prince, "Poor Australia! I devoutly hope they are ready for that pair. Unless, somewhere along the voyage, they find a congenial port.''

"Unlikely, me lads, since the little brig that carries them so snugly is owned by Samson Croft.''

The old man shuffled around, marking his retreat with his cane. Without looking back, he gave them his valedictory.

"I've no care for either of ye. It's Miss Jasper. I wish naught but good for the lass. She was never feared of the old ogre, not even when she was no higher than a harebell.'' And he left them.

Sir Desmond hesitated, then loped after him. He caught Samson Croft on the staircase and escorted him out to the square, though the old man made it clear he wished to be alone.

While the prince watched them from a window above, he heard Hannah come into the room. He swung around, feeling suddenly that his life had begun. All else was a prelude.

Pale and shaken as she was, she looked more welcome to him than the greatest beauty in Christendom. She came to him smiling, with her hands held out, but he crushed her fingers between their bodies, holding her close, almost afraid to let her go beyond his touch.

Sir Desmond broke in upon this idyl to announce, "He's on his way. Ruthless old beggar, though you can't but admire him."

Neither his sister nor the prince paid more than absent-minded attention to him, but he had his own thoughts to puzzle over.

"And to think I sympathized with that treacherous female! I'll never let myself be moved by a female's troubles again, I promise you, Hannah."

Hannah and the prince looked at each other, nodding together. The prince murmured, "Poor Fiona! However, I daresay you are right."

Hannah shrugged. "Poor indeed. I wonder what she will do when we are at home on our horse farm. Not that we must be concerned. Surely she has friends."

"Friends of good heart?" The prince considered the matter, only to dismiss it sadly. "She was too loyal to my family. A pity. She deserves better. But it is not to be."

Sir Desmond sighed, shook his head, and drummed his fingers on the wall beside him in a troubled way. Then he took out his watch and considered its face.

"I believe I have time to take out the phaeton for a bit of a drive. Why don't I leave you two to make your future plans while I get a little country air? My team will doubtless welcome the exercise."

"Splendid," Hannah and Prince Andre agreed together,

and Sir Desmond strode out, straightening his neckcloth and brushing back his ruddy hair with a much too casual gesture.

"How well we understand each other!" Hannah murmured, but was prevented from going into detail by the future horse-breeder's kiss.